"Kaye?"

In the shaft of light the open door let in, he saw something move under the bed.

He was on his knees and pulling her out the next second. "I'm here."

He lifted Kaye into his arms.

"Ready?"

She nodded weakly against his chest.

"Hang on," he said, and kicked open the cabin's front door...made a beeline for the trees.

"I can walk," Kaye whispered.

"Not fast enough." Even his strength and speed could turn out to be insufficient. He was running through unfamiliar terrain, while his pursuers probably knew every tree. He slowed only when he caught a small groan from Kaye.

The stain on her shirt was no longer brown; it was red now, soaked with fresh blood.

"I wasn't sure if you could come," she said.

"They would have to kill me to stop me." Didn't she know that?

DANA MARTON

PROTECTIVE MEASURES

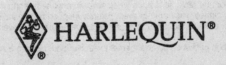
HARLEQUIN®

TORONTO • NEW YORK • LONDON
AMSTERDAM • PARIS • SYDNEY • HAMBURG
STOCKHOLM • ATHENS • TOKYO • MILAN • MADRID
PRAGUE • WARSAW • BUDAPEST • AUCKLAND

This book is dedicated with deep appreciation
to my editor, Allison Lyons, and to my family
for supporting me through the good times and the bad.

ISBN 0-373-88691-8

PROTECTIVE MEASURES

Copyright © 2006 by Dana Marton

ABOUT THE AUTHOR

Author Dana Marton lives near Wilmington, Delaware. She has been an avid reader since childhood and has a master's degree in writing popular fiction. When not writing, she can be found either in her garden or her home library. For more information on the author and her other novels, please visit her Web site at www.danamarton.com.

She would love to hear from her readers via e-mail: DanaMarton@yahoo.com.

Books by Dana Marton

HARLEQUIN INTRIGUE
806—SHADOW SOLDIER
821—SECRET SOLDIER
859—THE SHEIK'S SAFETY
875—CAMOUFLAGE HEART
902—ROGUE SOLDIER
917—PROTECTIVE MEASURES

CAST OF CHARACTERS

Kaye Miller—Majority Whip of the House of Representatives who's being targeted by faceless assassins. Instead of hiding in a safe house, she chooses to draw her enemies out. Could her decision cost her life?

Daniel DuCharme—Member of the SDDU, a secret soldier who fights terrorism, he agrees to guard Kaye as a favor to his commander. But what will happen when he starts to fall for Kaye, his commander's goddaughter?

Colonel Wilson—Head of the SDDU, reporting straight to the Homeland Security Secretary, and Kaye's godfather.

Agent Harrison—A Secret Service agent on Kaye's security detail.

Congressman Roger Cole—An old friend who seems to have turned into an enemy. He votes against Kaye every chance he gets, trying to undermine her career. How far is he willing to go?

Congressman Brown—He hated Kaye from the get-go. What does he have against her and is it enough to want her dead?

SDDU—Special Designation Defense Unit. A top secret military team established to fight terrorism, its existence is known only by a select few. Members are recruited from the best of the best.

Chapter One

Kaye Miller looked at her friends and colleagues milling around the grand ballroom, and wondered which one had tried to kill her.

Cold fear slithered up her limbs, along with a sense of bewilderment and betrayal. Who was it? And why? She'd only seen the shadow of the man's head through the car window, that and the Capitol Hill parking pass that marked him as someone close to her.

"Maybe next term," she said in response to a question from Congresswoman Sawyer by her side and scanned the crowd, considering each man in turn.

True, politics was a cutthroat business,

but she couldn't imagine any of these people as a coldhearted killer.

"If the wording was toned down—" She turned her full attention to Sawyer and made an effort to redirect her thoughts. "It shouldn't take much to get that little extra support you need."

"But I can count on your help?"

"You have my full backing." She was all for education reform.

Sawyer thanked her and moved on, leaving her alone and at the mercy of darker thoughts that brought images of crushed metal and screeching tires.

An accident, according to the police.

She wanted to believe them. She couldn't. She'd been there. The man had come after her with a purpose.

Would he come back to try again?

She absentmindedly rubbed the red plastic multiple sclerosis bracelet on her wrist, an accessory that almost every person wore tonight, including the men. Then she caught herself and dropped her hand. She didn't want to look nervous. She widened her smile and tried to focus on enjoying the evening. She didn't succeed. The lushly decorated room, the huge garlands of red roses and carnations, felt oppressive, as if the walls were closing in. And there were too many people. People she was no longer sure about.

Nonsense.

She was safe here, surrounded by at least two hundred politicians and media. Nobody would be stupid enough to try to get to her in this crowd.

Still, when somebody bumped her from behind, she jumped.

"Excuse me," a petite woman in a striking maroon dress said with a smile, balancing her drink and dessert.

Kaye stepped out of the way and let her by, tried to place her. She'd been skipping too many social events in the past two years. There had been a time when she would have known everyone at a gathering like this.

Sinatra's voice came faintly through the speakers, not meant for dancing, just loud enough to provide some pleasant background noise for the guests at the Multiple Sclerosis Society's Award Gala—everyone who had supported the vote for the newly approved research funds for the society. Tonight The Hotel George was as well-guarded as the White House.

And yet…she could not ignore the bristling of the short hairs at her nape, the distinct and disturbing sensation that she was being watched.

Wasn't she always? She was a public figure, Majority Whip in the House of Representatives. Thanks to C-SPAN and countless other news sources, people tended to recognize her. Even in this room where almost everybody knew her already, somebody might be keeping an eye on her, waiting for an opportune moment to come over and push his or her agenda.

Staying busy was good. She turned to join the group of men she'd recently scrutinized. Then she saw him: Tall and dark-haired, he wore a black tuxedo like every other man in the place, and watched her from across the room. Her, not someone behind or next to her—she was certain of that. His sharp gaze held her in a way so that she could swear she *felt* his attention. She didn't recognize him from the Hill, although he could have been one of the new aides.

Instinct said he wasn't. Not media either since he wasn't wearing a media badge. In a room full of all-smiles politicians, he seemed to stand alone with his sober intensity.

He didn't look away when she caught him staring. Why was he watching her? What did he want? Was it him? The man in the tunnel? She couldn't tell. She hadn't seen enough.

Who was he with? She thought she recognized the daughter of Senator Massey from Iowa, but the others she couldn't place. The people in the small group around him were chatting, but he didn't seem to be involved in the conversation. The older woman on his left put a hand on his arm and said something. He turned to her to respond.

Nobody. He was nobody important. She let out her breath. A guest, that's all.

Maybe a young representative who wanted to talk to her on some issue, but couldn't quite work up the nerve to approach the Majority Whip at a party.

And yet, he didn't look like someone who could be easily rattled. She watched him as he bent his head to listen politely to whatever the woman was saying. There was a strength to him, evident even at this distance, in his posture and controlled movements—a lot like Cal's.

She found the strength of strangers threatening just now. Kaye kept moving.

"Here you are." Norman Barney's weathered face lit up as he spotted her. "I was hoping we could discuss my little project. I want it in the hopper as soon as possible."

That's what she needed, some normal everyday conversation instead of standing alone and steeping in paranoia. "Agricultural easements?"

He nodded and steered her from the group.

She smiled and stifled the little voice in her head that screamed "anything but that!"

Norman Barney's voter base included a large number of farmers and he took representing them seriously. Nothing wrong with that, except that the man had a rather dramatic manner when he took the floor. A recent five-hour discourse on the proper processing of tripe came to mind.

"I'd like to hear your take on the upcoming presidential summit, too. It does affect my constituents. They depend on cheap labor from south of the border."

"We should be able to squeeze in a quick meeting next week," she said pleasantly. She wouldn't have minded a little work-related discussion, but she didn't want to enter into an argument right here, right now, an outcome that their opposing position on the issue guaranteed.

He waved that off. "Nothing that formal, Congresswoman. I was just hoping for a few minutes tonight. Just to sound you out."

"Kaye?"

The familiar voice had the power to lift the dark cloud that had seemed to hang over her all evening.

She turned with a smile. "I didn't know you were coming."

Cal was here. Nothing could happen to her now. Standing next to him was like standing in the shadow of a tank.

"Thought I'd stop by to say hi to my favorite goddaughter. Congressman." He nodded to Barney.

The man just about snapped to attention. Cal had that kind of effect on people.

"Colonel Wilson. It's been a while since we've seen you on the Hill."

"Retired." Cal let slip a half-smile.

"Getting some golfing done?"

"A little bit of this, a little bit of that. Mind if I steal Kaye for a few minutes?"

"No, no," Barney said. "I'll catch up with her later. Good to see you, Colonel."

"What are you doing here?" she asked as the congressman walked away.

Cal watched her closely with those dark eyes that others found formidable. "How are you?"

"Good as new," she said, but her hand fluttered to her left shoulder, dislocated in the crash in the tunnel. Nobody here, except she and Cal, knew about the accident. Her high-necked gown did a good job of covering the fading bruises.

"I had a little talk with your security detail," he said soberly, not missing the gesture.

He never missed anything.

"Thanks." If Cal gave some pointers to Harrison and Green, she felt that much safer.

"I want to bring in one of my own men."

She raised an eyebrow in response. Supposedly he no longer had any men in his command.

"From my old team. I managed to maintain a few contacts," he said with convincing innocence.

As far as anyone knew, the Colonel had retired a couple of years ago, only doing some light consulting now and then. Right. He was up to his neck in something, but no matter how much she itched to figure out the mystery, in the interest of national security and their friendship, she always accepted his explanations.

She wasn't about to start questioning

him now. "They're already whining about the security I have." She kept smiling, in case anyone was watching. "I'm not going to get budget approved for more. The police don't think the accident was anything deliberate. They think the other driver might have been under the influence."

"You won't to have to worry about my guy. If anybody asks, tell them he's a friend of a friend from the private sector, doing a favor."

"Okay." She couldn't see any reason why that shouldn't work just fine.

"I want him to go home with you tonight."

The buzz of conversation rose and ebbed around them. Crystal rang from impromptu toasts.

"You think it's that serious?" she asked, her temporary sense of safety dissipating.

"Just being overprotective." Cal's smile widened, crinkling the ebony skin on a strong face that otherwise showed little sign of age. "As boring as retirement is, this is the closest I can get to intrigue and action. I can't keep myself from meddling," he said and scanned the crowd reflexively, as he did every few minutes wherever they were. She was used to oddities that had been part of him since she remembered.

The next second his attention was back on her. "The cops are looking for the car?"

"Without success so far." She had no doubt he would get a copy of the final police report the minute it was completed.

"Good, good." He took her hand and patted it in a fatherly gesture. "Let me find the boy and I'll bring him over."

"If I'm talking with Congressman Barney, feel free to interrupt." She watched him walk away and melt into the sea of people—at fifty-two, he cut a finer figure than most men half his age.

Flashing cameras caught her eye to the right, the press talking to the senior representative from Illinois. The media hadn't made their way to her yet tonight, but they would sooner or later.

Better touch up the makeup; she'd been nervous enough to perspire. She navigated toward the bathrooms, greeting most people by name as she passed among small groups.

Norman Barney's wife was sitting on the pink sofa in the foyer of the bathroom, two women she didn't know chatted at the sinks.

"How are you, Alice?" she said as the door swung closed behind her.

"Good. Thank you, Congresswoman. New shoes." She pointed ruefully to her feet with a diamond-glazed hand.

Kaye smiled with sympathy. The heavy gown she'd chosen for maximum coverage was killing her.

Alice winced as she stood. "I suppose I better get out there. Almost over anyway."

"Almost." Kaye reached for her evening bag that held her lipstick and compact, then she changed her mind and went into a stall instead, sat on the closed lid. She needed a moment, just a few seconds alone to close her eyes and let her facial muscles relax.

"See you later," Alice called out.

The door closed with a swoosh behind her, then after the other two who soon followed, their voices fading as they gushed about some plastic surgeon. The buzz of people filtered in from outside, but blissfully muted. She had as much quiet as she could hope to get in this place. She rubbed her temples. How long had she been in here? A minute or two? How much could she afford?

Nothing escaped notice in this town. If the Majority Whip spent half an hour in the ladies' room at a major event, people would speculate. By tomorrow, the tabloids would either give her a deadly disease or accuse her of carrying the president's secret baby.

She allowed herself another minute or two before she straightened her spine and stood. Makeup, some more schmoozing, picking up a new bodyguard, then she could go home. If she couldn't drum up enough support for Tuesday's vote tonight, she would go in early on Monday and work the phones.

She was about to stand when the outer door opened and someone came in. Shoes scuffed the marble tiles—not the clicking of designer heels worn by every woman in the place. The scent of a man's cologne cut through the lemony smell of bathroom disinfectants.

Whoever was out there shuffled forward then hesitated. Should she say something? Let him know that she was in here and he was in the wrong place? Instinct kept her silent. The picture of the tall stranger who'd watched her earlier popped into her mind. Had he, or someone else perhaps, followed her in here?

She held her breath and pulled up her feet, careful to make sure her gown didn't dangle to the floor. She balanced on the top of the toilet, feeling stupid after the first second or two. Who was she kidding? If the man meant harm, all he had to do was check the doors and find which one was locked then he could shoot her right through the thin panel of wood.

The thought jarred her. This was ridiculous. She'd been watching too many crime shows late at night. Nobody was going to shoot her in the ladies' room of The Hotel George with half of Congress outside.

Still, her hand trembled as she stood

and reached for the door to pull it open. The outer door of the bathroom opened at the same time.

"Roger?" She glanced from the man to the young aide who'd stopped in her tracks at the door, then back again to Congressman Roger Cole, the House Majority Leader, who stood in the middle of the ladies' room with confusion on his face.

Tension left her at once, replaced by embarrassment. She had half worked herself into panic over Roger. She had to snap out of this. She couldn't be seeing boogeymen behind everything or she would drive herself crazy.

The Majority Leader blinked and his right hand came out of his pocket with a white handkerchief. He wiped his forehead.

"I apologize, ladies." He blinked again, then slid down to one knee.

"Roger? All you all right?" She helped him up.

"Too much champagne," he said quietly to her and offered a sheepish smile. "I'm sorry."

The aide was looking at him with a scandalized expression. She didn't recognize the young girl. To which party did she belong? It might make the difference in whether they would have to worry about seeing the story in the newspapers in the morning.

"Is your heart giving you trouble again? Should I call Liz?" she said distinctly, making the issue a medical one.

Until recently, Roger had been one of her strongest allies on the job, and beyond that a friend. But in the last few weeks, they'd had a couple of spats—just never could pick the same side of any issue. She had planned on talking to him when she found the time.

Tonight, he seemed subdued.

"It's not as bad as that, Kaye." He patted her shoulder, acknowledgement and appreciation glinting in his soft brown eyes. "Just got a little dizzy. I guess I didn't pay enough attention to the picture on the door, that's all. I suppose my mind was on other things." He pulled himself together, nodded to the aide still standing in the same spot.

"Thank you for your help, ladies. I apologize again. It's probably better if Liz and I call it a night." He glanced back at Kaye.

She nodded, trying to figure him out. She'd never seen him overindulge in alcohol before. Then again, lately she felt as though she no longer knew the man, as if he'd gone through a personality change—it was not just that he opposed her on nearly every issue, but the way he did it. If she didn't know him better, she would have thought he was deliberately trying to undermine her. The closer she got to becoming Speaker, the worse he became. Did he want the position for himself?

Working in politics had a way of making friendships difficult. You did the best you could and lived with the consequences.

Kaye looked in the mirror and saw the young woman go into a stall behind her. Another moment of solitude. She schooled her face back into the pleasant, reassuring smile she wore in public like a uniform. She washed her hands and dried them, touched up the smudges under her eyes with some powder, reapplied her lipstick.

She had to get a grip. She'd gotten scared half to death by Roger, for heaven's sake. Best thing to do was to go and find Cal. She'd feel safe next to him and get a chance to meet her new bodyguard. Whoever it was, if Cal had picked him, he was the best.

She exited the bathroom and nearly bumped into Roger again.

"Are you okay?" Did he need help finding his wife? Maybe he really was ill, and not just from the champagne.

"Feeling better," he said.

She took in the sheen of sweat on his forehead. "Is Liz around?"

"Ran off to say goodbye to a friend of hers." He glanced at his feet then back at her. "I heard what happened to you the other night. Be careful, Kaye. There are a lot of psychos out there. Make sure you're protected. You have good security?"

The concern in his eyes seemed genuine.

"Secret Service. Standard procedure."

He waited a beat, hesitated, then said, "There she is." He nodded toward the middle of the ballroom.

Liz was waving at them. Kaye waved back.

He put a hand on her arm, looking as if he was trying to find the words for something, but when he spoke, all he said was, "Better get going. You take care."

"You, too, Roger."

She stayed there for a second or two after he moved off. Something was going on with him. For one, the man never sweated. He was stressed, obviously so. Was he having trouble at home? At work? With drinking?

Or was she just desperately trying to find something to focus on other than her own troubles?

"SHE SURE looks nice." Daniel DuCharme took in the way Sylvia's crimson silk gown hugged her curves, transforming the no-nonsense ex-marine into one hot mama.

The Colonel snatched his attention from his secretary, looking for a moment as if he'd gotten caught in the act of doing something he wasn't supposed to. "She is an exceptional woman," he said matter-of-factly.

"Yes, sir." Danny kept a straight face.

If the Colonel insisted on living in a state of denial, who was he to burst that bubble? You'd have to be blind not to realize how the man felt about Sylvia. Seeing her anew in that getup, Danny was quickly developing an appreciation himself. He looked away, knowing the Colonel wouldn't like it if he caught him ogling.

What he didn't know was, why on earth was he here?

"I have a favor to ask," the man said.

Okay. Here it came.

"It's a personal request."

That piqued his interest—not that he hadn't been curious already. The Colonel didn't usually ask members of his top-secret team to a ball.

"Kaye Miller." The man measured his words, his voice kept low. "She was in an accident a few days ago."

Danny waited, not yet seeing any

possible connection to him or the SDDU—the Special Designation Defense Unit of which he was a member and Colonel Wilson its commanding officer.

"It wasn't an accident," the Colonel went on, looking him sharply in the eye. "She is very important to me."

Is she now? Danny glanced at Sylvia. He'd always assumed Sylvia was very important to the Colonel. Could have sworn he'd felt the tension between those two. Hell, half the unit were taking bets on them—no disrespect to the Colonel. Kaye Miller, though, she brought a whole new twist to the game.

"You want me to look into it?" He could do that. He hadn't been assigned to a new mission yet. He might have a few days of downtime.

The Colonel shook his head. "I'd like to ask you to keep an eye on her."

"Covert surveillance?" The SDDU didn't get involved in that kind of everyday stuff unless major terrorist activity was suspected. "Have we got some new intelligence?"

The Colonel shook his head. "It's not like that. As I said, it's personal."

Very interesting. "She needs a body-guard?"

"Whatever you think is best. I just talked to her about it."

"What does she want?"

"To live."

A reasonable wish. Still, he didn't care for the whole personal protection angle. Waiting and watching, that's all it would be and for nothing most likely. He'd rather overtake an enemy stronghold any day of the week.

But it wasn't every day the Colonel asked a personal favor.

"For how long?"

"Until we figure out who tried to spread her on the tunnel wall."

That sounded serious. "Didn't hear the story on the news."

"She managed to keep it out of the media."

"Must have taken some effort." Anything that happened to Kaye Miller was big news. She was one of the most influential women in politics, a beautiful widow recovering from a heartbreaking loss. She was the nation's sweetheart, and rumor had it she might just become the first ever female, as well as the first ever African-American Speaker of the House of Representatives sometime in the near future. At a damn young age for the job, too.

He'd seen her on TV and in the papers dozens of times, but those images hadn't done her justice. In person, she had a fragility to her, a haunted look that belied the strength shown in her straight spine and assuring smile. He was just as big a sucker as the rest of the country. His protective instincts had been flying high from the moment he'd spotted her across the room.

He supposed that's why the Colonel had brought him along. Try to turn down helping her after he'd seen her, if he could.

"She's waiting to meet you," the man said.

Danny nodded. No harm in talking to her. He followed Colonel Wilson as he cut through the crowd, and wondered why someone would want to take out Kaye Miller. Everyone seemed to love her. Hell, even her political opponents had come out to support her after her husband's death two years ago.

Then the Colonel stopped, and there she was. *She looks smaller up close* was Danny's first thought as he returned her polite smile.

"Kaye Miller, this is Daniel DuCharme, a good friend of mine."

"Danny." He took her hand, caught the flash of surprise in her mahogany eyes, immediately masked, felt the brief brush of calluses on her palm and wondered how she'd gotten them.

"The Colonel says you'll be helping me." She looked at him with polite interest.

"Yes, ma'am," he said.

She asked no questions, no proof of experience of him. She must have known the Colonel well enough to accept his recommendation without reservations. Just how well was the question. He felt slightly affronted on Sylvia's behalf.

"I'll leave you to get acquainted. There's somebody waiting for me." The Colonel took Kaye's hand and squeezed it, warmth and love and worry undisguised in his eyes.

She watched him leave as if reluctant to see him go.

Damn. The Colonel and Kaye Miller. Who would have figured? Not a bad match, though, if he thought about it. The Colonel was the best man he'd ever known, and the Majority Whip one of the most intelligent and beautiful women in the country. God knew, she deserved a little happiness after what she'd been through.

Why did the thought bother him then? Because he'd been rooting for Sylvia for years? Or because when he'd first seen Kaye Miller across the room, he had felt a pull of attraction himself, an almost predatory instinct that had kept his attention glued to her?

"Would you like a drink, Mr. DuCharme?" Her speech was cultured, matching the rest of her.

In theory, he had nothing against classy ladies. In practice, he found them too reserved and high-maintenance.

"Sure," he said. "Why don't we walk over to the bar?" She'd better not have thought that he would fetch her a drink. He was to be her bodyguard, not her assistant.

But she moved along as if that was what she had intended in the first place.

In addition to the waiters who circulated with crystal flutes on silver trays, a full-service bar stood in the corner of the ballroom. He put his hand gently to the small of her back to steer her through the crowd, then dropped it casually when he felt her stiffen.

The lady didn't like to be touched. A shame, since she seemed to have been made for touching. None of his business.

"Where is your security?"

"Since the building is sufficiently secured, I've given them some time off. They'll be here to pick me up at eleven."

He didn't say what he thought of that.

She turned back to pay attention to where she was going. Her black hair was piled high on her head, a few corkscrew tendrils escaping to dangle over her neck. She had an exotic look to her. If he hadn't already known otherwise, he would have thought her Portuguese. He had a second cousin who'd come over from Lisbon a few years back. She had the same lightly tanned skin and dark hair. The similarities ended there, though.

Kaye Miller's slim back tapered into an even thinner waist, accentuated by the cut of her dress. His gaze slipped to the curves below and he swallowed. Fine, fine, fine. He couldn't see her legs under the long gown, but he would just bet there was nothing wrong with those, either. He could definitely see why the Colonel was attracted.

She stopped all of a sudden and faced him, forcing him to snap his attention to her big dark eyes that reflected a mix of trust and hesitation.

Something answered deep in his chest, cutting him off guard. Whoa. He damn well better back down—and now.

"Thank you," she said. "I just want you to know how much I appreciate your help."

He watched the first earnest expression he'd seen on her, going beyond her stock trustworthy-politician-slash-touch-me-not-I'm-a-widow look. For a split second, he could see behind the mask and found that he very much wanted to get to know the woman he saw there.

"Sister Kaye." A stalwart African-American man pushed through the crowd to get to her.

"Congressman Webster."

"I haven't heard back from you on my tax proposal yet."

"I'm working on my own."

"Yes, I know, but mine is specific to black Americans. I am sure you would want to support your people." His voice was on the smarmy side.

"All my constituents are my people, Congressman. I'm trying to get a tax cut for the owners of all low-income businesses to give them a chance to grow."

"I think we must remember, Sister Kaye, that a lot of our people voted for us. They deserve our special consideration."

"I thought the point was to end special

consideration and make sure everyone gets an equal chance."

The man's wide smile dipped into a grimace, but he remained polite. "Maybe I could stop by your office and try to convince you."

"Of course. Marge can give you an appointment." She sounded tired.

"I suppose you get asked for a lot of favors," Danny said after the man moved on.

"Everybody in this business does. I love this country with everything I have." She looked after Congressman Webster then back to Danny. "Our history holds wonderful things that make me proud beyond words, and it holds some unspeakably terrible things that make me want to cry. One does not cancel out the other. And yes, I know we can do better. That's why I am here."

The passion that stole into her voice surprised him. He had a cynical view of politicians.

"Sorry," she said. "I've had a long day. I didn't mean to sound defensive. I do like what I do. Some days are just more trying than others."

He'd bet. Attending an award gala to celebrate the progress against multiple sclerosis, progress that had come too late to save her husband, and listening to patient testimonies had to be hard. And all that on top of a harrowing accident. Yes, the congresswoman had had a few difficult days lately.

And like that, on the spot, he made his decision. Kaye Miller had a number of things on her plate he couldn't help with, but for as long as she needed it, he would keep her safe.

THE MAN who watched them from the shadows drummed his fingers against the side of his leg. He didn't like the looks of the guy who was escorting Kaye through the crowd. Who the hell was he?

No matter. Their little chat would end sooner or later. He waved on a waiter who'd stopped by with a tray of champagne. Too early to celebrate. But the night was long, and at one point Kaye Miller would be alone in it.

Chapter Two

Daniel DuCharme was sitting too close.

On the rare occasion when she had a security escort, they never sat in the back of the car with her. Of course, Harrison and Green currently occupied the two front seats. She couldn't very well be annoyed at DuCharme for not sitting on Green's lap all the way home.

Kaye closed her eyes. Was that too rude? She didn't feel like talking. The week had been even more exhausting than normal for the job. She hadn't gotten enough sleep since the crash in the tunnel, spending half the night thinking about it, hoping to remember something that might give the police a clue, waking up frequently when she did sleep, her shoulder throbbing with pain every time she rolled on it.

She took a slow breath and thought about the weekend that stretched before her and tried to relax. She gave up after a few minutes and opened her eyes. "I hope I'm not inconveniencing you, Mr. DuCharme."

"Danny," he said again, shaking his head. "No inconvenience. I'm happy to help."

He turned on a smile that brought a reluctant response to her face. As when watching some larger-than-life movie star on TV, whose on-screen presence and charisma comes through strongly enough to bring out a physical response in the viewer, she found that Daniel DuCharme had that kind of magnetism.

He was beautiful, although he probably wouldn't have appreciated that description. His features were intensely masculine, but not in a rugged, tough-guy kind of way. He was the type who would make teenage girls giggle when they passed him on the street.

The man could have made a killing in

Hollywood—or politics. Put that face and smile on TV and start counting the votes.

"How old are you?" The question slipped out, to her instant embarrassment. God, had she just asked that? If she'd learned anything from her work it was never to blurt anything. She'd spent years training herself to weigh carefully every word that came out of her mouth. She wasn't herself. The stress was getting to her.

"Twenty-nine."

"I'm sorry. That was none of my business."

He shrugged, curiosity in his eyes, humor playing on his lips.

She shifted on the seat, causing the ample folds of her gown to spill over his lap. She pulled back the fabric.

Twenty minutes. In twenty minutes she would be home and she could go to bed and forget about the whole evening, the whole week in fact, everything until tomorrow morning.

She hoped.

Then Sadie, her best friend from college, would be here around noon. She had a six-hour layover on her way to the Middle East. Not nearly enough time for catching up, but as crazy as both their schedules were, they were happy for that much.

"Do you have a security system?" DuCharme—his eyes dark blue blending into gray—watched her with a focused interest she found unnerving.

She named the security company.

"That's good." He nodded. "Shouldn't have any trouble augmenting that."

He was full of unquestionable confidence. It radiated off him.

"You should discuss these things with Mr. Harrison." She nodded toward the man behind the wheel.

"We'll take care of everything, Congresswoman," the redheaded agent called back, his voice deep and reassuring.

She liked that about him. Harrison was a fine bodyguard, a professional, in his late thirties, experienced, large-framed. He and Green made her feel as safe as was possible under the circumstances. Rarely had panic crept up on her as it had at the reception.

"The Colonel gave me a rough rundown, but would you mind giving it to me again? Just to make sure I didn't miss anything," Danny was saying.

She did mind. She was tired, and she needed some time to get used to her new bodyguard, a chance to grow comfortable around him. She nodded anyway.

"The crash happened Tuesday night, around midnight, on the way home from a friend's birthday party. I was almost out of the tunnel when a black van pulled up next to me and pushed me right into the wall." She swallowed, her heart beating faster as she recalled the confused panic of the moment.

"The Colonel said you didn't think it was an accident." The smile was gone from his face now, replaced with focused concentration, the patch of skin between his eyebrows furrowed.

"He kept doing it, wouldn't let up. And when I finally stopped, he sped away."

"You're sure it was a man?"

"I think so. I didn't see him. That's the impression I got."

He nodded. "Have you seen the van before?"

"I can't say. It looked plain. I was struggling with the steering wheel, couldn't pay much attention to anything else. And it was dark."

"But you saw the parking tag?"

"They're pretty bright."

"I don't suppose you remember the permit number on it?"

She shook her head.

He waited a beat. "Ever felt like you were being followed before the incident or since?"

She didn't like the idea—creepy. But she made herself think back.

"No. Sorry. I'm not sure I would have noticed. I'm usually rushing around, planning what I need to do next, where I need to be."

"Have you noticed anyone around you acting strange, out of the norm?"

Nothing beyond the sensation of being watched at the M.S. gala. And the person who'd watched her turned out to be him.

"I work on Capitol Hill. People act

strange all the time. Everybody has secrets. Everybody has hidden agendas. Most of the people are working some angle at any given time."

"Have you upset anyone lately?"

"I upset a lot of people on a daily basis, but I don't think I upset them enough to want to kill me."

He kept on with the questions, and she answered each. He was thorough, no doubt about that. And slowly she let down her guard and started to feel safe with him, perhaps because of his demonstrated thoroughness or perhaps because he was one of Cal's men.

The hour was late enough for traffic to be easy even in Washington, D.C. They reached the tree-lined street she lived on in less than half an hour. Harrison pulled into the garage and she reached for her door, but DuCharme put a hand out to stop her.

"Hang on. Let me look around before you get out. Wouldn't want any surprises."

She stared at him, swallowing her flash of impatience with the delay. She was home, for heaven's sake, in her own house. But she was too tired to have a talk about expectations right here, right now. Tomorrow she would set aside some time with the three of them, make the new guy understand how Harrison and Green were handling her security, find a way he could help.

She dug up her keys from her evening purse and held them out for him. "This one." She pointed. "The security code is—"

"I'll guess. It'll add to the excitement," he said, ignoring the keys, and was gone in the next second, slipping into the darkness of the side yard.

Oh, for heaven's sake.

She leaned back on the leather seat, holding on to the keys. The phone number for the security company was in the drawer of the hall table. She could call them to let them know it was a false alarm when he set off the system. Still, he was bound to wake up the whole neighborhood. She looked into the night through the large window in the back of the garage. Should she ask Green to go after him?

"Who the hell does he think he is?" The man murmured under his breath, and, as if hearing Kaye's unspoken thought, got out. The overhead light of the automatic garage-door opener reflected off his shaved head, the brown skin smooth. In that light, from that angle, he looked a little like Michael Jordan.

Harrison was too professional to comment, but in the rearview mirror she could see him roll his eyes.

The agents had their own procedures. They always checked the doors for signs of forced entry and always went in ahead of her—Harrison walking through the rooms for a security check while she waited with Green just inside the door for the all clear. Their system had worked just fine so far.

"Tomorrow we'll sit down and talk about how Mr. DuCharme could contribute his experience and time," she said. She appreciated that Harrison and Green hadn't challenged the new guy just yet, probably mindful that she'd had all she could take for one day.

"Maybe we can—"

She stopped talking when DuCharme came through the door that linked the garage to the rest of the house. She stared for a moment. Guess he knew something about security systems. She was too annoyed with him to be impressed.

"Everything is okay," he said with a grin. He pushed the button to close the garage door before coming over to open the car door for her.

She followed him inside, shaking her head silently as she went. "Help yourself to anything in the kitchen. The coffee is up here." She opened a cabinet then closed it. "I'm going to turn in for the night. Thank you all for your help today. Good night."

If that sounded too much like a retreat, she didn't care.

She headed up the stairs without looking back, kicked off her shoes as soon as she got into her bedroom. She closed the door, opened her window then sank onto the bed, resisting the temptation to fall over and succumb to sleep. A quick shower first to relax her aching muscles, then some rest. Thank God it was Friday. At least she didn't have to worry about getting up early in the morning.

She unzipped her gown then stood and let it slide off her body, enjoying the cool night breeze that caressed her heated skin. The voluminous creation of brocade had way too much material for a midsummer party. She shed her panties and bra and tossed them into the laundry basket, picked up the dress to place it in the dry-cleaning pile. She could hear the men talking downstairs, a low murmur of masculine voices.

Daniel DuCharme.

She hoped Cal knew what he was doing.

The man was awfully…everything. And young. She was thirty-five and feeling much older. Working in politics added five years easily, losing her husband another five. It annoyed her that she cared. She shouldn't. She'd seen Secret Service agents younger than DuCharme.

But she hadn't been physically attracted to them. The thought stopped her in her tracks.

God, she was a fool. A surprised fool. She hadn't expected ever to feel that kind of awareness again. She'd thought she'd buried all that with Ian. Apparently not.

Ironic how those impulses would surface at the most inappropriate time with the most inappropriate man. Her body didn't care, she supposed. It had been neglected for a long time and it was letting her know it was still alive.

Part of the recovery process, probably. She had accepted Ian's death and dealt with the grief. She had to, or die with him. Nobody could live with that much heartache. She'd chosen to go on. But she expected the rest of her life journey, or at least the next many, many years, to be solitary.

She shook her head. She was too tired, her mind not thinking straight. DuCharme was her new bodyguard, nothing more, nor would he ever be.

The extra man would come in handy. She'd been feeling guilty about the hours required from Harrison and Green, although at least they didn't have to be on duty when she was on Capitol Hill. As long as she was inside, that location was secure enough. The rest of the time, the men divided the job into shifts, during which the resident bodyguard didn't let her out of sight. It would make things easier to have those hours divided by three.

She turned on the water and let it wash over her, let the heat relax her muscles. She always took hot showers, as hot as her skin could handle, even in the worst heat of summer. Ian used to tease her.

Ian.

It seemed impossible to have that closeness again with someone else—her body's sudden awakening in DuCharme's presence aside. She couldn't think seriously about him that way, not for a second. But someone else: a quiet, gentle, older man. Someone who would settle for what was left of her heart.

Maybe it wouldn't be that bad to have someone around again, someone who noticed the funny little things that made life theirs and unique.

She tried to picture some man in his

forties, a settling presence. Somebody who wouldn't make her wish for impossible things like youth and passion. She tried to think university-professor cardigans and hair that grayed at the temples.

She kept coming up with the picture of Daniel DuCharme.

DANNY KNOCKED on the bedroom door. No response. He tried the doorknob. Unlocked. He knocked again, louder this time, then pushed in the door.

Kaye Miller was just coming out of the bathroom, wearing a short terry robe that left her legs bare. *Kaboom.* They didn't disappoint.

There was a slight—very slight—twinge of guilt that he would notice such a thing under the circumstances. After all, he was here to protect her. Still, he was a man. He would have had to be dead not to notice, not to want.

He forced his attention above her shoulders. "Sorry to bother you."

"Is everything all right?"

"Yes," he said, as he slipped back into

bodyguard mode. "I was just wondering which of the guest bedrooms you wanted me to take."

Her mahogany eyes widened for a second then she recovered nicely. "The guards—" She cleared her throat. "Mr. Harrison and Mr. Green don't usually come upstairs."

"I'll have some equipment." He needed his tools to be able to do his job right. "I don't want to leave things all over your living room."

There was a quick flash of relief, masked immediately with a polite smile. "Of course. Pick whichever room you'd like."

"Thank you. I'll be gone for a little while to get what I need." He pulled a card from his pocket and handed it to her. "It's my cell number. I should be back in an hour or so. Mind if I take the Mustang?"

He hadn't brought his own car, had wanted the opportunity to talk to her on the way home from the party. And he wanted to get a feel for the Mustang anyway, should he need to drive it in an emergency.

"Of course," she said. "The key is on the peg by the garage door."

She stepped forward and took the card from him, but didn't look at it. She was probably uncomfortable with his presence in her bedroom. Oddly, so was he. Too bad. They weren't done yet.

"Does anyone have a key to your house? Parents? Boyfriend? Housekeeper?"

"My housekeeper," she said. "My parents are gone."

"I'll be changing the locks. I don't want anyone to have access until this current situation is resolved."

"The doors…" She hesitated a second. "The front door is really old."

An antique. He nodded. That was the trouble. Anyone with a hairpin could pick it. "I'm not going to damage it. You can have everything back to normal as soon as this is over."

She didn't respond.

"I know increased security is inconvenient, but it could be worse," he said, trying to lighten the mood. "You could be president." Then it occurred to him that she very likely wanted to be president. She was on her way, wasn't she? Man, she was way out of his league.

"I do appreciate your help." She folded her arms. Her robe slid a few inches down her shoulder from the movement, but she didn't seem to notice. "Can I help you with anything else?"

"No," he said, even though he had a list of questions. They could wait until morning when she was dressed.

He had to be losing his edge. Since when did he let a patch of skin get to him? Rafaela flashed into his mind, a Brazilian model, the girlfriend of some serious South-American badass whom he'd kept under surveillance last summer by hiring on to be Rafaela's bodyguard. Rafaela had the lovely habit of not wearing clothes inside the walls of the villa, a habit he enjoyed but wasn't particularly affected by.

Two square inches of Kaye Miller got him hotter under the collar than three months with Rafaela. "Good night," he said. "We'll talk in the morning."

"Did Mr. Harrison come up with a schedule that's workable for you? The rotation I mean," she called after him.

He stopped at the top of the stairs and looked back. "We left the rotation as it was. I'll be here 24/7."

She blinked. "All the time? You said you just needed the room for the equipment."

"I'll be sleeping on the couch downstairs. It's better-positioned." He prepared himself for a list of objections. The pet peeve of every bodyguard was people whose life was in danger but who resisted protection.

"You think it's that bad?" she asked instead.

"I don't know yet."

Unlike the majority of the cases he worked, he didn't have a file on her, hadn't had a chance to do any research. He would remedy that at the earliest opportunity. "I'm not taking any chances."

She thought for a moment, and he expected she might complain about the imposition. But when she spoke, all she said was, "Thank you, Mr. DuCharme. Good night."

Danny, he wanted to remind her as he drummed down the stairs, but shrugged it off. She would have plenty of time to get used to him.

He set the existing security, went out the back door, checked the perimeter of the property again, reconsidered the number of censors he would need. He crossed between the flowerbeds and watched Harrison and Green in the Town Car in front of the house. They looked alert, keeping an eye on the street. Good.

Danny stepped out of the shadow of a hemlock. They spotted him within a few seconds, nodded to him. Kaye Miller should be okay until he got back. He had asked both men to stay on duty until morning.

He hadn't told them he would be back before that. He wanted to test them. The stakes were too high to settle for an untried team. Quickest way to mess up an operation and get killed was not knowing the limits of the men you were depending on.

He went to the garage, checked the silver Mustang for tracking devices and found none. He hadn't expected any. If it weren't for her statement about the Capitol Hill parking pass in the other car, he would have dismissed the case as random violence. Was the attacker really someone from the Hill? Or was there a chance that Kaye Miller's own tag had reflected off the other car's window?

First thing in the morning, he would head over to the police lot that held the wreck and check it over.

He pulled out and cast a last glance at the house then took off to get his bag of goodies. He would secure the place, find who was after Kaye Miller, and maybe somewhere in between there, he'd have some time to figure out the woman—from a strictly professional point of view.

When it came to the personal side of things, he might as well call the mission Operation Hands Off. Aside from the obvious obstacles, she belonged to the Colonel.

KAYE DOZED, keeping an ear out for Ian's labored breathing. She'd spent countless nights like that, in the lightest of sleeps, her senses attuned to the signals of the ravaged body of the man she loved.

He breathed. Everything was well. She dipped a little further into sleep, her muscles relaxing.

Ian breathed. Something pricked her instincts. The breathing came strong and even, not at all like Ian's shallow struggles for air. The oddness of that, and something else, brought her awake.

She knew it had been just a dream before she even fully opened her eyes and saw the bed empty next to her. The familiar pain welled up in her heart.

She wanted to go back to the dream, back to Ian, even if just for a moment. She closed her eyes. The sense of loss was so acute just then, it burned her throat. A second ago in her dream, she could have reached out and touched him, snuggled with him, heard his voice. Maybe if she fell asleep right away, she could still go back to that place. Sometimes it happened.

There was the breathing again. She stiffened instead of relaxing into it. She wasn't dreaming. The breathing was real, closer now. There was somebody in her room.

She was facing the other side of the bed, the sound coming from behind her. She stayed still, against the instinct to turn. The new guard? She'd told him she didn't like the security guards upstairs. At the least he should have knocked. Or did she not hear it in her sleep?

Daniel DuCharme. He didn't seem like the type who would sneak into a stranger's bedroom to watch her sleep. If Cal said he was okay, then he was. But if not him—

In a split-second decision, she flipped and rolled across the bed, dropping to the floor instead of landing on her feet as she had planned. There was a small pop somewhere behind her.

"No!" She was trapped in the blanket.

Not for long, but long enough. The man was next to her already. What moon came in the bedroom window showed nothing but a ski mask. He was tall and thin, a gun in his hand.

"What the hell?" He swore at her as he shot again and missed.

She didn't recognize his voice. Where was her security detail?

She rolled under the antique four-poster bed, clear through to the other side. The bedroom door was closer to the attacker than to her. He'd get there first. He was already coming. She darted into the bathroom and locked the door behind her just as the man's shoulder slammed into it.

"Why are you doing this?" She didn't expect an answer, nor did she get any.

Where was everybody? She had three bodyguards. How did she end up alone with a murderous maniac?

She could have used a phone. No way to get to the one on the nightstand. She looked around for anything she could use to protect herself. Soaps, shampoo, lotions, towels, hairspray—she grabbed the latter, tucked it into the waistband of her pajamas and pushed the chair, the only movable piece of furniture against the door.

She opened the window and looked down to the tile patio a good twenty feet below her. Were she downstairs, the security system would have gone off. The upstairs windows didn't have any sensors. Could she jump? Only as a last resort. Even if she didn't break her neck, and chances were good that she would, she'd probably break at least a leg. If she couldn't run away, being down there wouldn't be much use. He could easily pick her off from the window once he broke through the bathroom door.

She leaned out as far as she could. "Help!" she screamed at the top of her lungs. "I need help!"

Why wasn't anyone coming?

Normally, she would have either Harrison or Green. Whichever man was on duty usually spent some time sitting in the car out front, making his rounds around the house every half hour. Tonight she had both agents—she'd seen them from her bedroom window before she'd gone to bed. The night was warm. They would have the car window down. Would they hear her? Or were they talking, distracting each other?

The door shuddered behind her again

and again. She needed a weapon. What? She had nothing remotely usable in the bathroom. She pushed into her walk-in closet. There. If she could rip the clothes bar out of the wall…She yanked off everything, dropping suits by the armload on the floor, and grabbed the bar, braced one foot on the wall. The braces didn't even budge.

Pop. Pop. The man outside the door was shooting at the lock. She didn't have long.

"Dear Lord, help me." She glanced up as she pulled harder, desperate, and saw the small panel in the ceiling. The attic. No dropdown stairs, unfortunately. They'd never used the place for anything.

Kaye ran back and grabbed the chair. The lock was still holding the door but just barely.

"My security is coming. Go away!"

She rushed to the closet. From the chair she pushed the panel open, pulled herself up—no light up there, no electricity at all, she would have to manage in the dark.

She looked down at the chair. Couldn't leave that. It would negate any advantage she had gained by coming up here. She hooked her knees over the ledge and dropped her body down. If she had a moment to think things over, she would have never done it. As it was, she had to act on the first idea that popped into her head, no time to look for a saner one. She stretched out all the way, her arms hanging low, her fingers brushing the chair's back.

God, was she really doing this? She had no coordination. Zip. Zero. People only did things like this in the movies. Even there, they used body doubles.

She wiggled. Another inch and she would have the chair. Either that or she would fall and break her neck. She stretched and got a firm grip, pulled herself up with the chair and set it aside. Apparently, desperation gave you wings. She'd barely rolled away from the hole when the bathroom door burst open.

She scampered blindly into the darkness, tripping on beams. The attic went on forever. Then her head smacked against something. The roof sloped. She reached the end and crawled into the corner, felt around and came across the brick chimneystack, squeezed in beside it.

Where on earth were Harrison and Green? What time was it? Had DuCharme ever made it back?

She could see nothing but the shaft of light coming up from below, the only sounds her own breathing and the thumping as the man jumped again and again to reach the opening. And then he did, blocking the light for a moment.

He came up, stood still for a few seconds, looking around.

"You shouldn't have run," he said. "You shouldn't have run."

She was in the shadow of the chimney, the darkest spot in the dark attic. Could he see her? Panic rose, her breath coming in ragged gasps. Could he hear that? She could hear him move around as he hunted her, the rustling of the insulation, the small bumping sounds when his shoes met a beam.

She wanted to ask who he was, why he wanted to hurt her. She kept her mouth shut, knowing he was unlikely to answer.

All she would accomplish by talking would be giving away her location.

She waited, willing her breathing to slow, ignoring limbs that were going numb from the lack of movement. The hot attic made her sweat, fiberglass insulation sticking to her naked arms, pricking them. She itched all over, but didn't dare as much as flex a finger to scratch.

How long could she hide up here? Had anyone heard her cry for help?

He stopped some twenty feet to the right, facing away from her. What was he doing? Probably listening. He hadn't seen her yet.

"You climbed too high," he said. "Somebody has to take you down. It ain't right, that's all. You've gotta be reasonable and admit it ain't right."

Was he insane?

If she could somehow get around him and get to the door…No. The second she moved, he would get her. He still had the gun. He was moving again, coming her way.

She needed a weapon of her own.

Nothing up here, but the two of them. And the hairspray stuck in the elastic of her pajama bottom.

She waited in silence.

He moved slowly, listening, checking every nook. He was getting closer and closer. She could hear him breathing, which meant he was close enough to hear her. She opened her lips to breathe through her mouth. Slow breath in, slow breath out.

They barely had six feet between them.

Then his head turned suddenly, and she could swear he was looking right at her in the darkness.

"There you are," he said, and stepped closer.

She gripped the can, flexed her muscles, getting ready to jump. And when he was close enough, she lunged from her hiding spot, going for the gun with her right hand while spraying his face with the hairspray in the left.

Chapter Three

He knew something was wrong as soon as he pushed through the neighbor's bushes and spotted Harrison draped over the steering wheel. SDDU jokes about the Secret Service aside, no way would Harrison be sleeping.

Danny ran the rest of the way to the Lincoln, saw the blood on the man's temple. He reached in through the driver's-side window and checked the pulse—faint but steady.

He flipped open his phone as he dashed for the house.

"Daniel DuCharme. Officer down. Requesting backup and a bus," he said, using the standard law-enforcement jargon for an ambulance, and gave the address.

The front door was locked from the inside. He went to the back, gun in hand.

A quick scan of the property showed it empty. Where was Green? Oh, hell. He spotted the man sprawled behind the large air conditioner unit. Danny crouched and felt for sign of life. None. Green hadn't been as lucky as Harrison.

Waiting for backup never even crossed his mind.

The back door opened silently under the pressure of his hand. He stepped into the kitchen and stilled for a moment, listening. The house stood silent, lights still on in the kitchen and hallway, same as he'd left it. No sign of struggle.

"Congresswoman?"

All his senses were on alert as he moved from room to room then up the stairs. He hadn't thought he was going to find Kaye Miller sleeping peacefully, but when he finally made his way into the bedroom, the sight of the empty bed was like a fist in the stomach.

She'd either been taken or there was a body somewhere else in the house.

He hadn't seen the basement and the garage yet.

He had lost her, damn it. He had lost her within hours of taking on the assignment. He sure as hell didn't want to be giving that news to the Colonel. And the cold feeling that spread in his stomach went deeper than professional frustration.

Fury came in waves. He was mad at whoever had gotten in here and at himself, too, at least as much. He shouldn't have left. He kicked at the bullet casings on the floor. No blood anywhere. That didn't mean she was alive, just that they hadn't killed her here. Still, as long as he hadn't found the body there was always some hope.

Something thumped above, and he jerked up his head. What was that? Then it came again, the sounds of struggle. The attic. He knew just where the door panel was, had noted it on his first run-through of the house.

A jumble of clothes covered the closet floor. He trampled them without thought as he jumped for the edge of the opening in the ceiling. He pulled himself up and, flipping on the flashlight he'd carried on his belt, saw the two figures rolling on the floor in the far corner and ran for them.

"Stop! Hands up! Kaye?"

They went on as if they hadn't even heard him.

He couldn't shoot. They were too close together.

He dropped the flashlight so he could grab for the man. The guy's head came up suddenly and smacked into his right elbow, making him drop the gun. He caught it with his left hand on reflex, shoved the man away from Kaye with the other hand and shot. The attacker was moving now, fast, tumbling away from them in the darkness.

"Kaye?" Why wasn't she talking? She had to be alive. He'd seen her move just a few seconds ago.

He glanced back at her as he rushed after the man. She wasn't getting up.

"Kaye?" He slowed, even though fighting instinct pushed him to go after his opponent, put him down until the man could no longer come up.

He squeezed off another shot at the silhouette that darted across the dark attic, then turned around and went back to Kaye. He picked up the flashlight and got the beam on her in time to see her sit up.

She was okay. He caught his breath. She was okay.

"I'm a little dizzy." Her voice sounded hoarse, her hands coming up to rub her neck.

"Are you injured, Congresswoman?" He kept his back to her, shielding her with his body, his head half turned so he could keep an eye both on her and on anyone who might come at them.

She reached for his arm. "Somebody was in here. He was choking me."

"I know." He panned the attic with the flashlight but it was empty save for the two of them.

"He had a gun. It's here somewhere." She glanced around frantically. "I knocked it from him, but then I couldn't find it."

"You disarmed your attacker?" That would explain why the guy wasn't shooting back.

He turned the flashlight at the floor and found the weapon hiding in the pink insulation. A Beretta with a silencer. He left it there for the crime scene team, not wanting to taint evidence. "Can you make it down from here?"

She was already standing and moving toward the light that came from below.

"Me first." He jumped down. "Okay." He braced his stance and caught her, then set her on her feet.

She wore silk pajama shorts with a slinky matching top. But far from enjoying the view, it filled him with hot anger. Her left shoulder was covered in old greening bruises, her neck and arms red with fresh abrasions, finger marks where the attacker had grabbed her.

"I should have been here." What the hell had he been thinking? He'd made the mistake of underestimating the situation and overestimating the men who had guarded her. And his mistakes had nearly cost her her life.

She didn't respond—probably too shaken. When she reached for the light switch, he put a hand on hers to stop her. "Let's not give anyone a target," he said. "In case there's someone out there."

Her hand trembled in his.

"Come on." He pulled her forward. "You need to sit down."

He led her to the bedroom with his gun raised, walking in front of her. The room was empty. He was pretty sure the rest of the house was too by now. Unless the attacker was exceedingly stupid, he would have taken the fastest way out.

She sank onto the mattress, and he grabbed her robe from the chest at the foot of the bed then wrapped her in it. "Are you okay?"

"Are you going after him?"

He wanted to. More than anything, he wanted to catch the bastard and pummel him a little before he slapped the cuffs on. But leaving her wasn't a good idea. Not until backup got here, by which time, of course, it would be too late. "I'm staying with you."

She just about sagged against him.

"Thank you. And thank you for coming back in time."

He said nothing, not happy with his performance. He hadn't expected a second attack, and certainly not this soon.

She shivered next to him. The night was balmy, but the shock of the attack was probably getting to her. He picked up a light blanket that lay discarded on the floor and slipped it around her shoulders, spotted a small picture on the floor and picked it up. He rubbed his thumb over the bullet hole in the frame. The photograph looked old, showing two young, uniformed black men.

"Your family?"

"My grandfather." She pointed to the man on the right. "And this one is Cal's father." She took the picture from him and set it on the dresser. "They were Tuskegee Airmen together."

"No kidding? Is that how you and the Colonel know each other?"

"Cal is my godfather."

His body was alert, his mind one-hundred-percent focused on the sounds of the house, on guard against any possible attack. But in a separate compartment somewhere inside him, something relaxed and opened.

"The Colonel is a good man," he said.

"Yes, he is." She clutched the blanket together in front of her, but the dark shadows of her bruises were still visible on her neck.

"Would you like some ice for that?" He pointed.

"It's not that bad."

It was. "When the paramedics get here, we'll have them take a look at it."

"Where is everybody? Where are Mr. Green and Mr. Harrison?" She looked up abruptly as if just now remembering.

"Harrison is injured. Green didn't make it. I called for help when I got here. They should be here soon," he said.

She turned toward him, her eyes round in the darkness, her lips trembling. "What do you mean didn't make it? What happened to Mr. Green?"

"Shot."

"Dead?"

She braced her elbows on her knees and buried her face in her hands, her hair falling forward. She didn't say anything.

He wanted to put his arms around her, but it seemed wildly inappropriate. And it probably wouldn't be adequate either. A man had given his life for her. He knew what that felt like and remembered the teammates he had lost over the years. She would need time to deal with the idea.

"He was doing his job. We all know what we're in for when we sign up for an assignment," he said, knowing he could take away neither her guilt nor her grief.

"Where is Mr. Harrison? Can we help him?"

"He's in the car."

She got up and went to the window. He pulled her back. "You can't leave the house, and I'm not leaving you. From what I could tell he just got knocked out."

He pushed her onto the bed gently and decided to do the only thing he could and try to distract her.

"Did you recognize anything about the man who attacked you? Body? Voice?"

She shook her head. "I was barely awake at first. Then we were up in the attic and it was too dark to see. The voice didn't sound familiar."

"As soon as the police get here I'll have them dust for prints."

"I want to know who he was and why he is doing this to me." Anger stole into her voice. "What did Mr. Green die for? I want to know." The last word was said on a restrained sob.

"You will." He would see to it.

She was not leaving his sight again until the attacker was dead or in custody.

"WHY ARE we coming down here?" Kaye picked her steps with care on the steep staircase. "I don't think we should—"

"The house is crawling with Secret Service and D.C. cops. It's a good spot to be out of the way."

Daniel DuCharme flipped on the light, and she stepped off the last step after a moment of hesitation. She hadn't been down here in ages. Both the workshop half and the gym portion of the single large room looked eerie, like a forgotten kingdom of dreams.

There had been a time when she'd hated to come down because the memories the place brought were too painful. The basement had been Ian's domain. It took more than a year, before she could look at his things without crying.

Now the place was just a room.

Her new bodyguard checked out the exercise equipment. She never used it, didn't have the time. The stack of weights gleamed on the carpet. Her housekeeper kept everything dusted and vacuumed. She was a gem. Kaye pushed in one of the hand weights to bring it in line with the rest.

He was watching her. She could see him from the corner of her eyes. She adjusted another weight and nearly knocked it off the rack. He was making her nervous. Ridiculous.

She turned to him. "Did you have more questions for me?" Better to face him than start acting like a jittery idiot.

"Sorry," he said. "I was staring."

Something had changed since last night, something she couldn't put her finger on. There was another layer to what passed between them. *What? What was different? Did he still feel guilty for leaving her?*

He could join the club. Guilt was eating at her over Green and Harrison.

She watched Danny. Last night his mood had been as dark as the attic where she'd fought for her life. Not now, although she could still see some of the tension in him. But it seemed he had compartmentalized the events of the night so he could go on with his work. She'd do well to follow his example.

He bent his head then looked up with those breathtaking eyes. "You know, you're the most famous person I've ever guarded. I've seen you on TV a million times." His lips stretched into a semblance of a smile.

He'd watched her on TV. A lot of people did. No reason the thought should fluster her.

What was it with them this morning? Maybe the danger they had shared the night before had brought them closer. Maybe it was that he was the only person in the house she knew. All the agents upstairs were new to her case.

"Do you do this often? Work as a bodyguard, I mean." She could have written the book on sounding and appearing composed and dignified. She could handle him.

"Most of my assignments don't involve protection."

What did they involve? Surveillance? Infiltration? Espionage? She didn't ask. Knowing that he worked for Cal gave her a fair idea.

"Nice setup," he said just before the silence became uncomfortable, nodding at the universal gym next to him.

"You're welcome to use any of this." Was that why he'd brought her here? To ask?

"Thanks." He paused. "Actually, we're here for you."

That took her by surprise. "You want me to work out?"

Great. He'd brought her here to whip her into shape? She looked down on reflex then snatched her gaze up, feeling stupid.

He wasn't interested in the circumference of her thighs, for heaven's sake. He probably thought she was too old to look at that way. He just wanted to help her take care of herself.

He leaned against the bench press. "I want you to learn self-defense."

She glanced at him then away, feeling uncomfortable with the suggestion. She could have handled a couple of pushups, improving general strength and whatnot. Self-defense training involved touching.

"My security detail was just doubled. I'm not really good at this kind of thing. I spend most of my life behind a desk."

She wasn't a very physical person. The whole flight into the attic had been a fluke. She'd been able to do it because she hadn't had the time to think about it.

"You fought off your attacker for several minutes, long enough for help to get to you. That was excellent. With some training, you could do even better should you need to next time."

There can't be a next time. She panicked at the thought.

He seemed to read her. "Two attacks don't happen on a whim. Someone set a goal of taking you out and they're working on achieving it."

"We've been ill-prepared before. I think now—"

"Stand over here," he said, and when she did, he grabbed her arm without warning and pulled her to face him.

Her heart hammered in her chest. In some recess in her mind she realized he was waiting for her to fight, to prove that she knew what to do. She couldn't. She froze.

He let her go after a few seconds, and she stepped away, annoyed at him for testing her, mad at herself for not rising to the challenge. He'd taken her by surprise. And the whole thing felt too weird. Did he really expect her to hit him?

"What are my most vulnerable spots?" He stood with his feet apart, watching her closely.

Her gaze dropped to the fly of his pants then bounced back up. "The male organs," she said. She was *not* going to let herself be rattled by this.

"What else? If you had to fight me off, where else would you hit me?"

All she knew about fighting was what she'd seen in action movies. "A right hook to the jaw?"

He gave her a lopsided grin that made him look even more handsome, and she felt a sudden unreasonable wish to be young again. She brushed it aside. She'd gone through all these years without making a fool of herself in the public eye. She wasn't about to start now.

"That only works if you have the strength to put behind it. You'd just bust your knuckles." He shook his head. "Think, Congresswoman."

Given the circumstances, the formality between them seemed unnecessary. "Kaye. Why don't you just call me Kaye?"

"And you'll drop the Mr. DuCharme?"

Her brief nod brought another smile to his face. She steadied herself and answered his earlier question. "The stomach?"

"That's good, especially if you have a weapon that's hard enough to ram in there, or if you're on the ground and can kick with your feet. Your thigh muscles are one of the largest in the body. You angle your feet right, and with your back braced on the floor, you can deliver a pretty good kick."

Her number-one strategy for any kind of attack was to run like the wind. If she was on the ground, it meant things weren't going well. Still, now that she'd been there, under an attacker who had tried to kill her in her own attic, she could value the advice.

"What else?" He pushed on.

"Legs? Hook the legs from under him?"

"Might work. If you can come at him from above, a good kick at the knee might break it backward, too. You'd be surprised how fast that'll stop someone."

Her brain immediately supplied what that would feel and sound like, and she flinched.

"No rules, no limits," he said. "You'll do whatever you have to. If you're close enough, rolling on the floor like last night, you can go for the eyes. Especially if anyone has his hands around your throat."

He stepped closer and placed his thumb gently in the inside corner, right by her nose.

His skin was warm and he didn't press, but still a shiver ran through her. Could she do that?

"No rules," he said again as he dropped his hand. "Trying to pry off an attacker's fingers won't work. Remember, you're getting less and less oxygen, getting weaker and weaker. Anytime there's any injury to the eye there's a powerful reflex to protect it. You shove your thumb or finger into the man's eyes, his hands are going to come up on instinct. It'll give you a chance to breathe, knee him, hit him, maybe inflict enough pain to get away."

She nodded hesitantly. The things he was saying made sense. And he wasn't trying to get her to do anything fancy, just a few simple moves. Still, she felt uncomfortable. She was ready to go upstairs and get out of the intimate seclusion of the basement.

He had not been threatening, rather the opposite, but he had paid closer attention to her, touched her more than any man had in a long time. She wasn't ready for it.

"The windpipe is a good spot, too." He lifted his chin to show her the exact place. "If you get a chance to punch it or kick it hard enough to crush the thing."

Uncomfortable or not, she had to pay attention. Her life might come to depend on it. She tried to picture herself whacking someone in the neck. Could she do it? Would she remember it if the moment came? The struggle in the attic flashed into her mind, cold fear squeezing her heart. She hoped she would.

"Okay then." Danny rolled his neck. "Let's practice. Let's pretend you're trying to get out of here. What do you do?"

She moved toward the stairs. He blocked her way. He was half a head taller than she, not massively muscled but wide-shouldered with an easy fluidity to his strength. When she tried to go around him, he blocked again. She lifted a hand, but couldn't make up her mind exactly what to do with it.

"Go ahead, you can push me," he said.

She did. Fast. She didn't dare hesitate and notice the way his chest felt under her palm.

The next second she was spun around, her back pressed to the very chest she'd been trying to ignore, both of Danny's arms locked around her. She froze again, just like the first time. She'd had all kinds of security details before, but nobody had ever manhandled her like this.

"Now what?" he said next to her ear.

She brought an elbow back and touched it tentatively to his chest.

"You'll have to do better than that."

"I don't want to hurt you," she said, flinching at how stupid that sounded.

"We'll take the chance." His tone was laced with humor, his grip tight.

She brought her elbow back with more strength and met a solid wall of muscle.

"Not bad. Now this time do it as if your life depended on it." He tightened his grip and pressed against her, his hot breath on her neck.

And she could feel again the way the man in the attic had pressed her into the uneven floor. She felt the panic of the dark. She jammed her elbow into his ribs as hard as she could, then the other one in a rapid second strike. She tried to bring her heel up to kick him where it counted, but there wasn't enough room.

He loosened his grip, but not by much. "Now we're getting somewhere." His voice wasn't exactly strained, but his tone wasn't as flippant as it had been earlier. "If his head is directly behind yours, you can try smacking your skull into his face. You might break his nose," he went on.

"Gross."

"You turn squeamish, even for a second, and you're dead. You're not going to get a second chance."

She nodded.

"Good. So you break his nose. Then you could lift both arms to the side and drop your weight. Do it as suddenly as you can. If you're on the ground when you get free, roll to your back immediately and kick the testicles, hold nothing back. When he doubles over, kick the head—chin, nose, anything is good. Use maximum force."

She dropped as he'd said and succeeded, although she was pretty sure he'd let her for the sake of practice. She ended up in a crouch at his feet.

"If you come out like that, step forward as you move up to give yourself some room. Don't waste time on trying to turn around fully, just turn your head. Bring your right foot up, heel into the groin. Again, when he bends over, kick his head hard. The second he's slowed down, run as fast as you can."

She moved forward as she stood, turned her head.

"Let's not waste each other's time. Do it like you mean it," he said.

Fine. She kicked as hard as she could.

He blocked it effortlessly, but doubled over to give her a chance to practice the follow-up kick. She did her best. He moved out of the way in the last fraction of a second.

"Okay, now I'm going to show you what to do if someone grabs you face to face, and a couple of other things. Then we're going to practice them."

They did. He wouldn't let her stop until her T-shirt was soaked with perspiration and she was gasping for air.

"Your stamina needs work, too," he said with arms folded over his chest as he watched her, looking as rested and relaxed as if he'd been an observer for the past hour instead of an active participant. "You should get on the treadmill when you have some time."

She took a deep breath and said, "I need a shower," instead of biting out the retort that burned her tongue.

He'd shown her an area of incompetence and she didn't like it. She liked knowing what she was doing. She enjoyed being the best. In politics, she'd worked hard, sacrificed whatever she had to, to get where she was. She wasn't used to feeling inadequate.

But he was right. She did need a lot of work when it came to self-defense. He was right, and she was grateful that he cared enough to tell her things she didn't want to hear. In her position, that didn't happen a lot. He was here to save her life, not to make her feel good. She would do whatever he said.

She moved toward the steps, but once again he blocked her way, shaking his head.

"You're going to have to get through me," he said with a cocky smile.

She was irritated enough to fight him as if she meant it. He blocked every punch, every kick. In a flash of frustration, she brought her heel down on his toes with full force, letting loose a cry that was downright savage.

God, that was embarrassing.

They both went still.

"Good. I didn't teach you that. You remembered the no-rules rule. You're learning." He grinned and stepped aside to let her by.

"You don't work like the other agents," she said as she walked up the stairs, feeling foolishly proud of herself all of a sudden.

He watched her with a calculating look. "As far as the new men are concerned... How do you feel about cutting back a little?"

"You don't think we need this many?" She stopped to look at him. "Mr. Green was killed and Mr. Harrison is in the hospital. The two of them weren't enough, so I don't think four is overdoing it."

His facial muscles tightened. "Four men, five with me included, might scare off the attacker."

"Isn't that the point?" It definitely sounded like a good plan to her.

"It'll be just a delay. He tried twice, the last time with two Secret Service agents on duty. I think he's serious about this. More security is not going to put him off. He'll wait. When Secret Service decides the threat is gone and pulls back, he'll come again and get you. Bringing on heavy guard now will do nothing but delay the next attack."

"You think I should hurry it?" Was he crazy?

"Get it over with and catch the bastard. Make him think he has a chance and grab him, take care of him once and for all. A trap."

She liked the sound of failsafe-extra-security, bad-guy-getting-nowhere-near-her much better.

"You want to use me for bait?"

He kept his keen gaze on hers. "Something like that," he said.

"Cal and I talked about a safe house this morning." Cal had brought it up, and she had said no, but now she wanted to know how Danny felt about it.

"A safe house would be great, but eventually you'd have to come home. What then?"

"Maybe by then he would be caught."

"Maybe." He hesitated. "I went to see your car earlier. There's very little to go by. Some smears of black paint, that's all."

"And the gun?"

"Unregistered. Impossible to trace. Not a fingerprint in the house either so far."

"So there's nothing?"

"There's always something. CSI is still working all possible angles."

"But you think a safe house would be a temporary solution."

"Unless we get a sudden breakthrough, this could turn out to be a very lengthy investigation. I'm not trying to talk you out of it. A safe house might be the best idea. You have to decide."

What would you do? The words were on her tongue, then she realized the obvious answer so she didn't ask. He wouldn't hide. Of course, he knew how to take care of himself. She didn't.

"If I went someplace safer, would your job...Would you come?"

"Yes," he said without thinking.

It made her feel immeasurably better.

He tilted his head. "Is that what you want?"

"No." She drew a deep breath to bolster her courage. "Let's draw that slimeball out into the open and end this once and for all."

He grinned. "You're tough."

"I have to be. I'm in politics."

"Tougher than that," he said. "It's one thing to stand up to arguments and negative campaigns. Standing up to a loaded gun takes a hell of a lot more guts."

The compliment felt ridiculously good, even if she didn't feel all that brave, only a woman with a limited number of choices.

"Kaye?" he said as he stepped closer. "I'm not going to let anything happen to you."

And there it was again, that acute awareness between them that made the air too thick to breathe. In the narrow staircase, his face was close enough to touch, his blue-grey eyes deep and luminous enough to fall into.

She could still feel his touch on her body as he'd guided her from move to move earlier.

I can't think like this. I can't feel like this.

"Thank you for the lesson," she said as she turned to run up the stairs.

When he called after her, she pretended not to hear it and kept going.

Chapter Four

The man sat down on the brown couch in the living room, squeezed his beer into the rip in the cushion. The yellow foam, more and more of which showed as the years went by, held the bottle in place.

He clicked on the TV and settled on the hunting channel, put his feet up on the stained coffee table. Damn faucet was dripping in the kitchen. He turned the TV up. Hell, he never had the chance to fix anything with all the time he'd been spending at camp and going back and forth.

That's all he'd been doing lately. Going to work, going to camp and, in between, when he had the time, figuring out how to get to Kaye Miller. He'd taken on the responsibility willingly, even though it took a back seat to the main objective. To the others in camp, Kaye Miller was of secondary importance. They had bigger fish to fry.

To him, Congresswoman Miller was everything.

She was the one who had ruined him. Her tax laws, damn woman. Women had no place in politics—never understood it, never would. Especially not one like her. No way was she going to be allowed to keep at it, to become Speaker of the House, third in line for the presidency. Over his dead body. Derickson was bad enough, worse excuse for a president he'd ever seen, but Derickson, too, would be dealt with soon.

"Let freedom ring," he said to the dog and rubbed his aching arm then picked up his beer and took a long draft. The attic had been rough. Damned bodyguard came out of nowhere. He'd seen the man leave and hadn't realized he would be coming back.

His stomach growled. He picked up the half-finished bag of beef jerky from the coffee table. The fridge had been broken for two months, maybe three. It would stay that way, too, for a while. Every penny that hadn't gone toward the mortgage he'd been kicking in for the camp.

"Git!" He smacked at the dog as she jumped on the couch and almost upset his beer. Then, because she obeyed, he threw her a chunk of dried beef.

The coffee table wobbled under his feet as he shifted his weight. Everything was falling apart.

Not Kaye Miller's mansion, though. That house had been just fine, with her fancy furniture and fancy security. But he had gotten in. He might not be rich, but he was smart, and he knew how to take care of business.

He would have, too, if it wasn't for the third bodyguard.

He pictured her right now, sitting on her leather couch, watching that big TV, probably eating a fine meal delivered from a real restaurant.

"It ain't right," he said to the dog and tossed her another chunk of food.

Kaye Miller better enjoy what she had

while she had it, because he was about to fix the injustice. He had found the means and found a friend who was willing to help. He picked the small vial of clear liquid out of his pocket and rolled it between his thumb and forefinger with a smile.

THE REPORTERS started to arrive around noon—not bad, considering. Her connections had gained her half a day. After that, nobody could hold the story back.

Kaye took a last look at the media gathered at the end of her driveway then drew the blinds and settled into her upstairs office. She glanced at the caller ID on the phone that flashed another number. She'd turned off the ringer on all the phones in the house hours ago. People had been calling since the first news report hit the airwaves.

"Majority Whip Kaye Miller's house under attack…unknown assailant…terrorists…" The stories and speculations got wilder by the minute. She switched off the small TV in the corner and sank into the relative silence. Much better.

It didn't last long. Her cell phone buzzed a minute later. The display showed her secretary's home number.

"I'm okay, Marge."

"Thank God. I was outside. Just came in and turned the TV on. If there's anything I can do—"

"Thank you. I'm fine. I'll probably be in a little early on Monday."

"Should I set up something for a quick press release?"

"Taken care of. Random burglary. It should be out in the next half hour. I hope this madness will die down after that."

"I feel like I should be there."

"It's Saturday. Do we have to have that you-are-entitled-to-live-your-own-life talk again?" She was joking, but Marge's loyalty touched her. "I'll be fine."

She spent another minute or two reassuring the woman that she was okay, then hung up and turned back to the computer screen in front of her, to a chat board for victims of a certain investigational drug therapy. She was planning on using them as an example in her patients' rights talk.

She tried to immerse herself in work, but found it hard to focus. Normally, unless she had some work-related emergency, she spent her weekends in her garden.

"Knock, knock." Danny stood in the open door.

"Are you sure I can't go out even just to the back yard?"

"You want to risk a sniper?"

"No, I guess the weeds are not worth it." He was right. She needed to be in here. But she felt antsy and could have used the soothing effect the plants and a few hours of physical work would have had on her.

"Don't you have a landscaping service?"

She shrugged. "Gardening gets me outside and moving around." Not having a service forced her to breathe a little fresh air now and then.

But her garden was more than exercise. It had become her haven, her therapy over the last couple of rough years. She'd started the first flowerbed as a diversion for her mind, something she could take care of that would grow instead of dying. Then she'd fallen in love with the lilies and peonies, grown attached to her dahlias. "I think I'm becoming addicted," she admitted.

He stepped into the room. "That explains the calluses."

She rubbed her palm, self-conscious all of a sudden about the rough patches of skin. "I tore out a bed of pachysandra a few days ago to make room for some mums in the fall," she said, then remembered that he'd probably come in here for a reason. "Do you need me for anything?"

"I'm thinking about making lunch. Can I interest you in some food?"

Did she have anything in the fridge? Normally, she went grocery shopping Saturday mornings. If she didn't get to it over the weekend because of travel or too much work she'd brought home, she left a note for the housekeeper who came on Mondays, and the woman took care of it.

"I can make lunch." She shut down the Internet. The man was stuck with her 24/7.

The least she could do was feed him. She hoped there was a can of tuna somewhere in the cupboard. "Do you eat tuna fish?"

"I was thinking bruschetta and mine-strone soup."

"That's fine. We can order in. My treat." There were a couple of Italian restaurants nearby that delivered.

"I can make it. Not much else to do. We're practically under siege."

"You cook?" She passed by him and padded down the stairs.

He took them two at a time and caught up, flashed her a disarming smile. "I'm what they call a full-service bodyguard."

Her mind took a little detour on that statement. She looked away. What on earth was wrong with her? What was it about him that reduced her thinking to the most basic, hormonal level?

"You don't have to cook. It's not your job to feed me," she said then turned into the kitchen and saw the grocery bags. "Where did this come from?"

"Delivery."

"We have that?"

"Almost all the big chains deliver." He smiled at her.

She looked back at the bags, at the loaf of Italian bread that stuck out from one, and focused on the aroma of the fresh bread instead of the thought that there were just the two of them in the house. The two new agents who had replaced Harrison and Green were outside, keeping the media at bay.

She wanted to go back upstairs and hated the cowardly impulse. "Can I help?"

"Sure," he said, watching her as if he could read every thought that flew through her head.

She hoped not. "How about this?" She pulled a pot, suitable for soup, from a base cabinet. "Want me to fill it up with water?"

He shook his head as he grabbed an onion from one of the bags and started to peel it. "A little olive oil."

She brought out the jug from under the sink, poured and set the pot on the stove. He came over to dump the onions in, then turned the burner on low.

"So where did you learn to cook?" she

asked, just to keep on talking, and watched him tackle a couple of cloves of garlic next.

Ian and she had never cooked like this together. Neither of them knew how. For the most part, the stove was used for cooking pasta on the odd occasion when they didn't go out, order in, or pop in a microwave dinner.

"I learned how to toss together a couple of meals in college to pick up girls." He admitted good-naturedly, looking just the tiniest bit embarrassed. "I'm afraid I was pretty shallow in my younger years. Had a one-track mind."

And now? She didn't ask, not sure if she wanted to know.

"This job must be hard on the social life," she remarked instead. Funny, that had never occurred to her with either Green or Harrison. Neither had ever mentioned their private life.

"No girlfriend to complain about it." His gaze was on her as he dumped the crushed garlic into the pot. "Keep stirring," he said.

She focused on that, until the monotonous task finally relaxed her. "What else do we need?"

She would *not* ask any more questions about his personal life or allow herself to make another stupid remark. She had been guarded by dozens of men over the years, but she had never let her guard down like this with any of them, had never let any this close. Nor would they have wanted to be. They were trained to be invisible and professional. Why was everything so different with Danny?

Because he was one of Cal's men. The trust she had transferred to him was instant and complete. Maybe that had been a mistake. She needed to pull back, if it wasn't too late already. Things certainly couldn't go further than this. She wouldn't allow it.

"Celery, carrots, herbs." He pulled the items from the bag as he named them. "Smell this."

She bent to the twig of rosemary he held up to her nose. "Nice." The sweet-spicy scent seemed to fill her head. She recognized the herb from having seen it used at restaurants as garnish, but other than that, she had little idea about what to do with it. She normally avoided the more "gourmet" sections of the grocery store.

He rinsed and chopped the celery and carrots, did the same with the herbs then dumped everything in.

"How do we know when it's done?"

"The onions will turn soft and see-through."

He pulled an eggplant and a zucchini from the paper bag. "While you were upstairs, I had a chance to look through some House transcripts for the last couple of months or so. You've taken some hits from the other party."

She shrugged. "That's the way the game is played."

"What bothers me more is that you took some hits from a couple of men on your own team. What's the story with Congressman Cole and Congressman Brown?"

"Neither of them would come to my house in the middle of the night to shoot me, if that's what you're asking. For one,

Brown has been in New York since Tuesday for his mother's funeral."

"Cole has a pretty good alibi, too."

She stared at him. "You questioned Roger?"

"Not yet." His eyebrows went up. "You didn't hear it on the news? Congressman Cole had a mild heart attack last night. He's been in the hospital."

Oh, God. "It's—" She shook her head. "That explains why he was acting so strangely at the awards gala."

"How strange?" Danny turned the tap off.

"Came into the ladies' room by accident. I was alone in there. I thought— I don't know what I thought. He spooked me. I didn't pay close enough attention. Now that I know…I think his heart was troubling him already. If only I—"

"You are not a doctor. You can't diagnose a heart attack before it occurs."

She couldn't. Still, if she was so preoccupied by her own troubles that she didn't pay enough attention to a friend—

"How come he votes against you on just about every issue?"

"We used to be on better terms. The whole Speaker thing…"

"You're moving up and he's not."

"I really don't want to believe that he could be like that."

"But he sure acts it?"

"Lately." She nodded. "Then last night— He seemed a little unwell, but nice again. You know what I mean? Said he heard about my accident. Told me to take good care of myself. He hadn't talked to me like that for a while."

"How did he hear about the accident?"

The question stopped her. News of the crash had finally gotten out after the attack at her home. The press of course connected the two and speculated wildly. But they had not heard at the time when Roger had talked to her.

"Did you tell anyone?"

"Cal and Marge my secretary. I had to reschedule some appointments. There were cops on the scene. An older couple stopped to help, but I don't think they recognized me. The people at the emergency room and my insurance."

"So he could have heard. I'll still check it out as soon as I can get in to see him," he said. "What about Brown?"

She shrugged. "He couldn't stand me almost from the get go. Not sure why. I know his wife. She's nice enough. Suze went to college with Ian. They went out for a while, I think. Suze invited us over once. I don't think Jack liked that. Rumor is, he's pretty jealous. And Suze is much younger than he is. I used to think he hated us because of Ian, but he hasn't eased up in the last two years, so who knows? Funny thing is, Suze adores him."

"Speaking of jealousy," he said slowly, with apparent reluctance. "It might help if I knew if either you or your late husband had any extramarital relationships."

"No," she said without thinking, appalled at the suggestion. How could he ask something like that?

"Have you had any relationships in the last two years that ended badly?"

She took a long breath. "I haven't—I've been alone since Ian." Not that it was any of his business.

"I'm sorry. I had to ask."

He *was* sorry. She could see from the way he was looking at her. But beyond the apology, his gaze held other things she wasn't brave enough to acknowledge—genuine concern, care, maybe something more.

She'd had good-looking bodyguards in the past. Why was she having so much trouble with this one? Why did she feel on the edge and all awkward around him? If her body was going to take notice of a man after all this time, couldn't it have been someone else? Someone who didn't work for her and who wasn't a much younger man.

Maybe she was going through the change early, she thought, and felt better having identified the problem. Obviously a horde of misguided hormones were trying to overtake her body. She wasn't about to let them. No matter what it cost her, she was going to act with dignity and decorum.

"I'll be in the living room. I'm going to check what they're saying on TV." The press release would be coming out around now—just the thing to distract her from Daniel DuCharme in her kitchen.

She made it as far as the couch before she saw the stranger in front of the sliding glass doors outside.

"Danny!"

What happened next was a blur of action, during which she ended up on the floor behind the couch, watching Danny leap across the room and shove the door aside. He took the man down roughly.

"Who the hell are you?" His gun was at the intruder's back, his right knee holding the guy to the ground.

"Press." The man could barely get the single word out, his face smushed against the bricks.

"ID." The gun didn't budge. "Don't move. I'll get it."

Danny reached around the man's chest and must have found what he was looking for, because he yanked and came up with an ID tag.

Just a reporter. She willed her heart to slow as she pushed away from the floor and started to stand.

"You stay where you are," Danny said without looking at her.

Agent Meyer burst through the front door at the same time. "Where the hell is he?" He had his gun drawn, came straight through to the living room. "Can't believe the idiot wouldn't listen."

"Taken care of." Danny hauled the reporter to his feet.

"Are you all right, Congresswoman?" Meyer was helping her up. "I'm sorry. They're going crazy out there. Everybody wants the story behind the story. We checked the lot of them, they're all clean, but they are a pain in the—" He took a breath. "I saw him come back here, but had to handle another one. And this one just wouldn't stop. Didn't want to shoot him in the back."

"No. That's okay. Everything's fine." The last thing she needed was a dead reporter on her lawn.

"Want me to take him out front?" Meyer asked Danny.

"I'll do it in a few minutes. Thanks." Danny was searching the rest of the man's pockets. "Call in that police unit we have on standby. They can take him in, maybe hold him for the day just to teach him a lesson."

"You can't do that to me," the reporter protested with outrage and tried to twist away from Danny without success. "I didn't do anything wrong. I just wanted to talk to the congresswoman."

But Meyer was already making the call.

She went back to the kitchen and sat at the table, next to the scattered ingredients that were still to go into the soup. What was in the pan smelled wonderful. She let the aroma of the spices soothe her, looked up at the sound of an approaching vehicle.

Flower delivery. She could see through the window as the van stopped behind the press line. For her? From who? Her birthday wasn't until next week.

She stood to watch as a young boy got out and went to the back, came away with a large bouquet of pink roses—her favorites. He was immediately stopped by the other agent out there. He looked as though he was protesting, pointing to his watch. Probably had a schedule to keep.

The agent patted him down and checked the flowers, but still wouldn't let him through.

"I'll get them for you, Congresswoman, once DuCharme comes back," Meyer said from behind her. "If you're okay here, I'll go and do a walk-around."

"Of course. Thank you."

He went out through the back.

She watched through the window as a police car arrived, saw Danny go up to it with the reporter, talk to them.

The flower delivery boy was talking to the agent again, looking sullen and worried. She wondered if he could lose his job if he was late with his deliveries.

She picked up the walkie-talkie from the counter. Which line was Mr. Dalton's? Channel two, she remembered and twisted the button. "It's okay. You can let him through," she said.

The agent looked toward the house. She waved the boy on from the window then opened the door for him.

"Thank you, ma'am." He was younger than she'd thought, barely old enough to work.

"No problem. It's not always as crazy around here as this."

"Signature on line twelve. You someone famous or something?" He handed her a clipboard.

"Politics."

The boy looked disappointed. "Where would you like the flowers?"

"On the counter will be fine," she said and shook the pen since it wouldn't write.

She grabbed one from the drawer in front of her, signed. "Here, you better take this." She turned to the boy. "Oh, not there. Here."

He was setting the flowers by the stove. She pulled them farther away where they wouldn't be affected by the heat and wouldn't drop any petals into the soup.

"Sorry," he said. "Thank you, ma'am." He just about ran on his way back to the van.

She closed the door behind him then went back to the vase and removed the small envelope from its plastic stick.

Danny came through the door. "Don't do that again." He went straight to the flowers and checked them thoroughly, then moved them out to the patio.

"They'll wilt in the heat," she called after him.

He pushed the vase a few feet over into the shade. "You should never let anyone in."

"He was just a kid. Mr. Dalton patted him down."

He shook his head. "Someone could have sent the kid to check out security. *Nobody* comes in. Mr. Dalton should know better than to let anyone through." He was opening his cell phone and dialing. "This is Daniel DuCharme from Congresswoman Kaye Miller's security detail. I'm calling to confirm that you have a reporter by the name of Tom Delinsky out here covering her story." He listened for a while. "Thank you."

He pulled the phone from his ear and dialed again. "This is Daniel DuCharme from Congresswoman Kaye Miller's security detail. I'm calling to confirm a delivery to…" He gave the address. "I need to know when it was called in, from what number, credit card information, everything you have." He paused. "Fine. I'll send someone with authorization to pick it up within the next twenty minutes." He closed the phone and put it away. "Why are you looking at me like that?"

"It's—I haven't had security this tight before." And she hoped she wouldn't need it long. She missed her freedom.

"If your security was tight, that reporter and that boy wouldn't have gotten as far as they did. I'll have to talk to the agents about that."

"I don't want them to shoot some innocent citizen for coming near me."

He waited a beat before he nodded. "Understood." He walked over to the stove and turned the burner down. "I'm going to step back out for a minute to talk with Dalton and Meyer. Stay inside and stay away from the windows. Please."

She reminded herself that he had her best interest at heart, and sat in the spare chair in the corner as the door closed behind him. She opened the card in her hand.

Hope you are all right. Happy early
birthday. Marge

Well, that was nice of her. She would
have to call and thank her secretary for
her thoughtfulness. Her gaze wandered to
the stack of bills and other miscellaneous
mail on the small desk next to her. She
rifled through them. All the envelopes
were open—Danny had already checked
them. By the time this was over, he would
know more about her than just about
anyone else. She wasn't sure how she felt
about that.

"Visitor." Danny was coming through
the door. "She says you were expecting
her?"

"Sadie!" She'd totally forgotten in the
craziness.

"So you do know her?"

"My roommate from college. Where is
she?"

"She should come back in a few weeks."

"Absolutely not. She can't. She's
leaving the country."

"How well do you know this woman?"

"Like my sister. She is coming in."

"Fine, coming in." Danny turned and motioned to someone outside. "I'll be a few more minutes." He stepped back out.

"What on earth is going on here? Have you just announced that you'll be running for president next?" Sadie Kauffman came through the door a few minutes later and smiled as she ran forward for a hug. "I've been on the plane all morning, haven't seen the news."

"I'll fill you in." Kaye squeezed back. "God, it's good to see you. It's been a while."

"Way too long."

"And now you're going away."

"Just for a year or two. Remember these?" Sadie handed her a bag.

She recognized the gold-striped paper box instantly. "Mario's canolis?"

"The one and only."

"God, I've missed you."

"Who are you kidding? You missed the canolis."

"Okay, that, too." She grinned as she put the box on the table. "Come, sit down."

"So, what's going on?" Sadie raised a perfect eyebrow.

"Had a break-in last night."

"Are you okay? Were you robbed?" She looked around.

"I think he wanted me."

"What?"

"He had a gun. We wrestled around for a while before Danny got him off me."

"Danny who?"

"Daniel DuCharme. The man who showed you in. He's one of Cal's, temporary addition to my security detail."

"One of Cal's?" The eyebrow went up again. "He's hot."

"He's young."

"He patted me down before he let me in."

"Sorry. He takes his job very seriously."

"Don't worry about it." Sadie winked and she stood. She always did have too much nervous energy. "I kind of enjoyed it." She went to the stove, looked at the soup. "Who's cooking?"

"Danny."

"Danny, huh? Interesting."

"Wipe that smirk off your face. He's just a kid."

Sadie stirred the soup then sniffed the wooden spoon. "Minestrone." She nodded her approval. "Smells great. How long before it's ready?"

"No idea. Half the stuff isn't even in yet."

"I suppose there's no sense in tasting then." She put the spoon back down and looked out the window. "Have I told you, my fifty-eight-year-old mother is dating a thirty year old? The other day I asked her what she liked about him. You know what she said? She said he had three outstanding qualities: stamina, stamina, stamina." She rolled her eyes. "How is that for embarrassing? Don't laugh at me. This is serious. My mother is a pervert."

"Sounds to me like she's happy."

"Well that, too. But it's— He could be my little brother." She sat back at the table and lifted the lid off the box. "Canoli?"

"Before lunch?"

"Life is too short to postpone desert."

Kaye smiled, the stress of the morning

melting off her. "God, it's good to see you," she said as she got up for plates.

"Same here." Sadie grinned back.

And it was as if they were still back in the dorm, eating Mario's canolis for breakfast, lunch and dinner, whatever time they could get their hands on a box. Sadie had always insisted that canolis were brain food. Of course, she would. Her mother was Italian.

"Did they catch the guy? What did he want from you?" she asked.

"He got away. He—" It hurt to talk about it. "He killed one of the men on my security detail and injured the other."

"Oh, my God." The first canoli stopped halfway to Sadie's mouth. "So he's some serious lunatic?"

"Probably. I should be okay now. Danny is pretty good at what he does. And Cal is helping, too. Plus the Secret Service and the cops. They're checking out every angle."

"Good. They better keep you safe."

"They will." Kaye took her first bite

and relaxed into her chair as the sweet cream diffused on her tongue. Mario was a god.

"So, um, about Danny," Sadie said after a while. "What is he, thirtyish?"

"Twenty-nine."

"He's no kid."

"I know," Kaye said and took another canoli.

"He *is* gorgeous."

She kept silent. She wasn't going down that road.

"And you're practically locked in the house with him all day." Sadie wouldn't give up.

"Come on, he's way too young."

Sadie watched her. "He is not, and we both know it. Question is, why are you trying to convince yourself so hard that he is? Could it be because you're attracted to him?"

"No. Absolutely not. And if I were, you'd be making fun of me like you just did with your mother."

"That's different. I don't like to think of

my mother having sex. There's just something weird about it."

"Better get used to it. She's probably having more fun than the two of us put together."

"Great. Depress me, why don't you?" Sadie made a face. "Anyway, you should take a page from her book. Would it kill you to have some fun?"

"Would it kill you not to meddle?" Kaye laughed. "God, didn't we have this conversation ten years ago?"

"And as I recall, you didn't follow my advice."

"And escaped Mel the Maniac."

"More like missed out on Mel the Magnificent."

Kaye groaned and rolled her eyes. "Enough about me. I can't believe you're going to Yemen."

"It's either that or sleep with the department head so he'll recommend me for his post before he retires."

"That can't be true this day and age."

"Sadly, yes. I swear the hospital has a thing about promoting women. Trouble is, all the candidates have about the same background. Two years of international experience with Doctors Without Borders should put me over the others, enough so I have a fighting chance for the position."

"And if something happens to you?"

"You're right here in the U.S. and look at what's happening to you. Who says any place is safe?"

Sadie had a point there.

"And Brian?" Kaye asked with caution.

"What Brian? The weasel-who-used-me-to-get-ahead-then-dropped-me Brian?"

"Right." No, there wouldn't be a chance of reconciliation there.

"I'm done with men. Don't laugh. I don't mean like I'm never going to have sex again done. I mean like, I'm never going to trust one again. It's a losing proposition."

"Come on, there are still decent guys out there."

"Like Daniel DuCharme? Is that why you can't deny the attraction fast enough?"

"It would kill my career."

"Would not."

"Can you see it in the headlines? Majority Whip, Widow Kaye Miller Caught in Torrid Affair with Bodyguard. There goes the vote from the religious right."

"You can't live your life according to the next vote."

"I don't. But I've worked awfully hard to get where I am. I'm not going to throw it away on a whim."

"You're too young to give up on happiness."

"I'm thirty-six."

"Thirty-five till next week," Sadie said. "Plenty young to find love again."

"I don't expect to find love again. I just want a contented life, doing the best I can at my job, maybe making a difference." She thanked God that the sharp, soul-tearing pain of Ian's death had passed, though sometimes she felt guilty about it. Love. She couldn't risk that again. Nobody could expect her to.

"Ian would want you to be happy." Sadie guessed her thoughts.

"I know."

"You can't bring him back by turning your back to everything that's fun. You don't have to stop living just because he can't."

"I know."

"Okay. I'm not going to badger you about it."

"Right. That would be way out of character." Kaye grinned.

"Way. Not like me at all. So as far as Danny goes, I want regular progress reports," Sadie said.

"He'll be gone as soon as they catch the guy."

"Uh-hum."

"You never give up, do you?" Kaye shook her head.

"Not in my nature," Sadie said. "It's not in yours either."

TWO O'CLOCK had passed by the time Sadie left for the airport. The media circus was gone. They'd moved on to a sex scandal that was unfolding at the IRS. Apparently, accountants were deceptively passionate under their cool demeanor.

Kaye reached for the paper box in the middle of the table, empty save for the chocolate smears.

Danny was looking at the damning evidence out of the corner of his eye as he stood by the stove. "I don't suppose you're hungry anymore?"

He'd stayed outside while Sadie was there, giving them some privacy, popping in only a few times to finish the soup and start the bruchetta.

Kaye inhaled the fragrance of basil. "I'd love a taste."

That was the trouble with Mario's canolis. They were light enough to have been made by angels. You could eat half a dozen and an hour later be hungry again.

"I talked to the Colonel earlier. He said to tell you he'll stop by tomorrow," he said as he ladled soup into two china bowls.

"Any other news?"

"Small progress here and there. Nothing that would give us enough information to make a move."

"So what can we do?"

"We wait. Our man will come back." He glanced out the window.

She could see Mr. Meyer in the car in front of the house from where she stood. Mr. Dalton was stationed out back.

"Any news on Mr. Harrison?"

"He's been released from the hospital. He wants to come back to your detail badly."

"Absolutely not, he needs to rest."

Danny hesitated as he set the plates on the table. "Might be good for him if he comes right back. He probably feels guilty for messing up on the job."

"He didn't mess up."

"That's not the way he would see it."

"In a few days." She set spoons and napkins next to the plates and sat down.

He stirred his soup. "Watch out, it's very hot," he said and took a spoonful and blew on it, tasted carefully. He made an odd face. "Might have put in a little too much rosemary."

"I'm sure it's just fine." She blew on hers, lifted the spoon to her mouth then realized she hadn't put any glasses or drinks on the table yet so she set her spoon down and got up. "Anything to drink?"

"Water would be fine." He took another taste. "Maybe it's the celery." He tried again then shook his head.

She put two glasses of ice water on the table then sat back down.

"Thank you." He looked up. "I was thinking. You should sleep in one of the guest rooms tonight."

The spoon stopped halfway to her mouth as a twinge of fear ran through her at the thought of the upcoming night, the terror of waking up to an intruder in her bedroom still fresh in her mind. She didn't want to go to sleep at all. "Whatever you think is best."

"I'm not going to let him anywhere near you. The upstairs windows are all secure now. There are sensors all over the place. I turned them back on as soon as the press left."

He'd had to turn off the system for the press. They kept stepping over the line, setting off the alarms.

She nodded and reminded herself that

this time he would be here with her, in the house. He would be guarding her all night.

She found comfort in the thought, in the meal they were sharing—such a domestic act. Maybe too much comfort. She must not get used to that, to him. Someday soon, when this case was resolved, he would leave. She must remember that.

She watched him eat, the way his sensuous lips closed around the spoon and his hair fell over his forehead. He looked up, caught her watching him and flashed a grin.

Something leaped in her chest in response.

He had brought something to her house, home cooking and sudden grins, a sense of being alive and aware, possibilities beyond work and schedules. She was going to miss that when he left.

She blew on the soup in her spoon. Whatever Danny said about the spices, it did smell wonderful.

"We are going to set up a trap," he said. "Leave him only one point of entry. I'll be waiting for him."

"You think he'll come back tonight?"

"Maybe. Or he might wait a few days for you to get comfortable and let your guard down. It doesn't matter when he comes. I'll be here and I'll be ready."

"It will be over soon," she said because she needed to hear it.

He nodded and put a fist to his stomach, made a funny face.

"You don't think so?" she asked.

"I do," he sounded breathless. "I just—"

The next second, he was doubled over, his soup spilled.

"Danny?" She grabbed for him, but too late. He went down with a groan, his knees touching down as his body swayed just before it hit the tile floor.

"Cramps." He pushed the word past his white lips. "Poison."

Chapter Five

"I hate this." Cal paced the kitchen while the crime scene team dusted for fingerprints yet again. "I want to take you to a secure location until we figure out what's going on."

"No," Kaye said. She wanted whoever was after her caught. No way was she hiding while Danny lay in the hospital. They weren't going to win. "I can't leave my job indefinitely." She had every intention of being at work on Monday. "If I run now, it will encourage every nut to try this before an important vote he wants to influence."

"What's happening on the Hill? Have you got anything coming up?"

"Patients' rights."

Cal paced. "Who's against it?"

"Big pharmaceuticals, insurance companies, doctors, you name them."

"Some of these people would have easy access to poison."

She nodded. She'd already thought of that, had a hard time picturing it.

"What else? What do you have in the next couple of weeks?"

"Export laws and lots of meetings that might lead to something or might not. Danny had already asked for the list. I think he was working on it with Secret Service."

Cal nodded. "I'll check up on that. You won't reconsider a safe house?"

"I mean to get my work done."

He flashed her a look of exasperation. "Congress is your career. This is your *life* we're talking about."

"If I disappear now, whoever is doing this will just wait me out and come after me when I come back."

"Not if we catch them first."

"And if you don't?"

The Colonel grunted. "How the hell did that boy get in here?"

"I let him in." She winced. "He was just a kid. He was in and out so quick. I couldn't have had my back to him for more than a second."

"That's enough. If you had any of that soup, it would be your stomach getting pumped right now. Or worse. The only reason Danny isn't dead is because he only had a taste of it." He fell silent for a few moments. "I'm pulling two of my guys off another job. It's going to take a day, maybe more."

Which meant, they were probably deep undercover in some vital operation. The impression she had of the Colonel's clandestine activities was that he was into something heavy and serious. The CIA came to mind.

"I don't want you to compromise national security for me," she said. "If you need those men elsewhere—"

"It's already done. They're coming."

"And until then?"

"Until then, you're going to have half the Secret Service camped out in your front yard."

God, this was going to be a media circus if she'd ever seen one. She steeled herself. It'll be what it'll be. There was no help for it. No point in complaining, either. She'd been lucky. If things had played out differently she could be dead by now.

Danny.

She couldn't put the picture of him out of her mind, the way his eyes had rolled back as the paramedics rushed him out. She had panicked. The blood still rushed in her ears when she thought of it. He had to pull out of this. He would. She couldn't bear considering the alternative.

"I'm staying the night," Cal announced, having come to a decision.

"I appreciate that, but—"

"No but. You're my one and only god-daughter."

No point to try to change his mind when he was like this. And to be truthful, she didn't mind the company. "Okay. Let me get the guest room ready."

His beeper buzzed and he glanced at it.

"Any news on Danny?" *Please God, let him be okay.* Pain like sharp metal sliced through her heart. Hadn't she prayed those words not so long ago for Ian? Prayed them in vain.

"It's something else," Cal said. "I'm in the middle of something." He thought for a second. "I'll stop by the hospital and check on Danny as soon as my men arrive and take over here."

"You can go now, if you want to. I'll be fine." She was desperate for news of him.

"I'm not leaving you."

"Then take me with you." She didn't feel all that comfortable in the house. She'd been attacked here twice in the last twenty-four hours.

"It's out of the question. Much easier to get to someone when they're moving around."

"They don't seem to have any trouble getting to me when I stay put. Can't you get me out of here without anyone knowing?"

He stared at her through narrowed eyes as a smile spread on her face. "That's not a half-bad idea. Get you off the premises and stuff the place with Secret Service. If the attacker doesn't know you're gone, he might come back. We could set a tidy trap. You can spend some time at my place."

She tried not to let her face show how little that appealed to her. Cal's space was…creepy, to say the least. On the other hand, however, it was built like a fortress. "So, how are you going to get me out of here?"

He waved over one of the men from the crime scene team. "I'm going to need your clothes," he said.

"Excuse me, Colonel?"

Cal pointed toward the downstairs powder room and gave his order. "Start stripping."

SHE HATED waiting, a personal disadvantage since politics was full of it. Nothing happened on time on the Hill. The same seemed to be true for hospitals.

A secret service agent on each side of her, Kaye tapped her feet on the white vinyl floor tiles outside Danny's room. His doctor was in there with him, and Cal. They'd only allowed one visitor in. What on earth was taking so long?

The air conditioner was going full blast. She was freezing. She'd taken off the sweatshirt she'd stuck under the overall to disguise her figure, and now she put the old thing back on, glanced down the hallway. She wanted to stop by to visit Roger, but she didn't want to miss the doctor, wanted to hear what he had to say about Danny. Shouldn't be long now.

A man came down the hallway with a clipboard. "Are you Mrs. DuCharme? I'm going to need your husband's insurance card."

"I'm Kaye Miller. Daniel DuCharme works for me."

The man blinked and his watery green eyes went wide. A second later his thin lips stretched into a smile. "I'm sorry, Congresswoman. I can't believe I didn't recognize you."

She returned the smile. For the most part, she preferred not to be recognized. News coverage for the long months after Ian's death, and the media's fascination with her ever since had made that difficult. And that was before she had agreed to be one of the spokespersons for the Multiple Sclerosis Society. The TV commercial that resulted had made her one of the most easily recognizable faces on Capitol Hill these days.

"Some of the tests we need to run are pretty expensive," the man said. "I'm going to need authorization from someone."

She shivered suddenly, rubbed her arms with her hands as she glanced at Cal through the glass. He was deep in discussion with the doctor.

"Whatever tests or treatments are necessary, if his insurance doesn't cover it, I'll be paying the bill," she said. It was the least she could do. The poison had been meant for her.

"In that case, could I trouble you with some paperwork, Congresswoman?"

Something about the man seemed vaguely familiar, though she couldn't recall meeting him before. His straight-as-nails, straw-colored hair and dark eyebrows—with the zigzag scar above them—made a strange contrast she would have remembered.

"I was hoping to catch the doctor when he came out," she said.

"This shouldn't take more than a minute. I'll just need your signature on a few forms. The office is down the hall. If Dr. Taylor gets out before we finish we'll see him walk right by."

"Of course." She went with him, the two Secret Service agents Cal had had meet them at the hospital following close behind.

The administrator stopped at the door of a small office that held only two chairs and a desk. The agents checked the room over then moved back to wait by the door.

"Please, take a seat. I hope you are all right. I saw what happened to you on the news. Crazy world, this is." The man walked around the desk and plopped down. He pulled a few sheets from his clipboard and passed them to her. "If you could fill these out—I'm just going to need credit card authorization."

She fished he card out and read off the numbers while he typed.

The printer next to her spit out one page after the other, about half a dozen in total.

The guy grabbed them up when he was done on the computer. "Let me make some copies."

He pushed aside a panel and walked through a door on the opposite wall, but didn't go far. She could hear him moving around in there. She could hear a copy machine come to life, whirring and clicking.

The picture on the desk caught her attention. Another man with a small child. Maybe a brother and nephew. Or life partner. On second look, the office was rather feminine, with more pictures—cats—and a small pink vase among the many knickknacks. Maybe he shared the office with someone. It wasn't any of her business. She clicked on the pen and turned her attention to the forms she was supposed to fill out. She made quick work of them and was done by the time the man stuck out his head from behind the door.

"If you're finished, you can just pass those to me and you're free to go," he said, then disappeared again.

"Thank you," she said, even though he'd

left the room. She grabbed her purse as she stood and then took the papers to him.

He was fiddling with the settings on one of the copiers in a small room that opened to his office on one end and to a hallway on the other. A second copier was going full force already with some giant job he'd just started, spitting out one sheet after another, filling the small room with noise. The place looked like a supply closet, save for the gurney by the wall that held a large roll of black plastic.

A body bag. She turned away when she realized what it was.

The other machine caught her eye again. The pages coming out of it were blank.

"I think you put the originals in backwards," she said without turning.

"I think everything is as it should be now, Congresswoman," he said and pressed against her in the small space as he moved forward.

And in that instant, as she felt the pressure of his body on hers and heard that voice close to her ear, low like that, she recognized it.

The man in her attic.

She opened her mouth to scream, but his hand was over it already. He punched her in the side with the other hand before she could twist away.

Not punched. She looked down confused and saw the handle of a blade sticking out, felt a sudden sharp pain that took her breath away. She went down fast, the noise of her falling swallowed by the whirring of the machine next to her.

The last thing she registered was the wet sound the knife made as it was withdrawn.

DANNY LOOKED DOWN the empty corridor and moved forward, both his anger and his fear tightly suppressed. He was in commando mode. No room for emotions, only precise, faultless execution. He would not stop, not feel until he accomplished his mission.

It was early evening, the visitors gone, and the hallways of Walter Reed Hospital were deserted except for the occasional nurse coming off or going on duty.

His knees seemed to be made of jelly. A

temporary weakness, he hoped. Man, having his stomach pumped had been rough. His throat felt raw. He ignored that and the slight dizziness, courtesy of the poison his body had already absorbed by the time the ambulance had gotten him to the E.R.

His mind was focused on a single thought: *Somebody took Kaye.* She'd been taken with two Secret Service agents waiting just outside the small office where she was supposed to sign paperwork. For him.

They had made the worst possible mistake—underestimated the enemy. She had to have been followed to the hospital from home. Then once they got here, the enemy had improvised. The man was good, whoever he was.

Where was she? And what had they done to her?

There had been blood on the floor of the room from which she had disappeared. Hospital security cameras had picked up an unauthorized transport of a body through the parking garage. He put the picture of the still body bag on the gurney out of his mind.

He had promised her he would keep her safe, damn it.

He passed the nurses' station, walked on until he found two older women stripping sheets off a bed in an empty room and stuffing them into a laundry cart. He flashed them his most charming smile. "Hi, I'm Brady White with the Secret Service. Congressman Cole is waiting for me, but I think I got lost. It's my first time here."

One of them smiled back shyly, a short stocky woman with gray hair that was cut into a boyish style. "He's one floor up. I'm going that way anyway. You can come with me."

"That would be extremely helpful," he said and followed her.

"Bring me a coffee, too, would you?" the other woman called after them.

"Of course." Rosa, according to her nametag, yelled back without stopping. She moved as if she had someplace to be, her shoes clopping on the floor. "He's just one floor up. You were close," she told him.

He nodded, putting on a grateful and relieved expression.

The key in these situations was not to ask anyone in charge. A nurse would have known the security procedure. House-keeping, whom most everyone ignored, were happy to show someone they thought important that they knew everything that went on in the building.

He made small talk while they rode the elevator.

"Sorry," he said as he bumped into her when the elevator stopped and they stepped forward to get off at the same time. "Please, go ahead." He smiled as he slipped her ID tag into his back pocket.

"Turn left at the end. Last room." The woman pointed down one of the hallways. "There's another agent out front. You can't miss it." She paused. "I can walk with you if you'd like."

"That's not necessary. You've been very kind. Thank you." He smiled again and turned from her, moving down the hallway slowly, allowing her time to walk down another corridor and pass out of sight.

When she was gone, he grabbed some soiled scrubs from another laundry cart—looked like it was housekeeping time on every floor—stepped into the nearest empty room and pulled the green garments over his clothes, clipped Rosa's ID on his breast pocket and turned it sideways as if it'd gotten brushed aside. He grabbed a clipboard from the end of the bed, tucked it under his arm and went on to meet his target.

No time to go through the proper channels and ask permission. Not when every minute could mean the difference between Kaye's life and death.

The Secret Service man by the door barely spared him a glance. He was there as a formality. The congressman hadn't been under any kind of threat. And Danny had picked his time well, the end of the shift; the man was tired and ready to go.

A few more steps and he was in, face to face with the congressman.

He sat on the edge of his bed and noted his gray complexion, his sunken eyes. "I don't work for the hospital." He pulled the call button, which the man was about to push, from his reach with one smooth movement.

"Relax. I'm not here to hurt you." He lifted his hand, ready to clamp it over the congressman's mouth if he decided to call for his guard. "I'm here about Kaye Miller," he said.

Cole turned even paler. "Has any-thing…happened to her?"

"You tell me." He pinned him with the same look he used to interrogate terrorists.

Cole looked away. A few moments of silence passed. "I'm sick. Look, I don't know who you are." He breathed unevenly. "Leave."

"I don't think you're a murderer," Danny said.

"Oh, God." Cole shrank into his pillow. "Is she dead?" He took in air in short gasps.

"I'm really hoping that she's not. But she *is* missing. Why don't you help me find her alive?"

Cole struggled to sit, not quite succeed-ing. "I didn't do anything." Gasp. "I don't know anything. This is outrageous." Gasp. "Who are you?"

What was he trying to do, kill himself? Danny pushed him back onto the bed. "Stay still. All you have to do is talk."

The man wheezed. "You're wrong. I'm seriously ill. You can't think I had something to do with this."

He could have made him talk quickly, as distasteful as he would have found strong-arming a sick man like that. For Kaye, he could have done anything.

"Who has Kaye Miller?" he held back for now.

"I don't feel good." Sweat beaded on the man's forehead. "Please. I need a doctor."

"How did you know that the congresswoman was in an accident?"

The man stared at him for a few seconds. "I can't...remember. I think she told me. No, maybe Marge told me. I don't know."

The monitor he was hooked up to showed rising blood pressure and heart rate. Damn it. He wasn't faking it. Did he have information? Was there enough suspicion to justify what Danny would have to do to make him talk?

There wasn't. All they had was Cole's voting record. Not enough to risk killing the man. Danny swore.

"I was never here," he said and tossed the call button back to him before he walked out of the room.

The guard at the door didn't even look up from the magazine he was reading. Danny couldn't blame him. He'd spent his own share of time on mind-numbing guard duty where his presence had been largely a formality. Now he loved the SDDU because their missions never lacked action.

And action was exactly what he needed now. He had to find out who had Kaye, then he had to go and get her back.

If Congressman Cole wasn't involved, then who? Danny strode down the hall. They had precious few leads. The only other man who had jumped out at him from the records was Congressman Brown.

He had bet on Cole. Who knew why he'd gone into the ladies' room? What he would have done if that aide hadn't shown up? His instincts bristled at the man, but even he could be wrong. Cole certainly didn't look in good enough shape to orchestrate multiple assassination attempts. That left Brown. The Capitol Hill parking tag pointed to someone in politics and these two seemed the most obvious. Not that he would ignore the rest. Sylvia was running all background info for the whole of Congress and all Capitol Hill employees, making a list of everyone with the slightest connection to Kaye Miller. Unfortunately, getting comprehensive and usable results would take a while, and Kaye had already been missing for three hours. She could be anywhere by now.

Danny walked outside and flipped open his cell phone. "Hello, Sylvia. Could I ask for a favor?"

"Always, and now more than ever," she said. "The Colonel mentioned you were working on finding Kaye. He's out of his mind with worry, drilling her Secret

Service detail right now. The agency is using all their available resources to find her."

"I'll bring her back." He would find her or die trying.

"What can I do for you?"

"I need an exact location on Congressman Brown. Kaye mentioned that he's in New York for his mother's funeral."

To her credit, Sylvia asked no questions. All she said was, "It shouldn't be too hard to find him."

KAYE FELT dizzy and weak, slowly becoming aware of the darkness and the plastic that was suffocating her. She clawed against it, registering the sounds and movements of a vehicle. The scene at the hospital came back in a rush, the man who'd called her into the copy room.

She desperately searched for an opening and found it, pushed a finger through the small hole at the top of the zipper and worked it down a few inches. She gulped a quick breath, then another as she tried to move around in the dark. She couldn't straighten her legs. A trunk. She was locked in the trunk of a car that was taking her God knew where.

She wiggled her fingers until the opening was wide enough to fit her hand through, then she grabbed the zipper and pulled it down as far as it went, pushed the bag off her head and shoulders.

The trunk was small and smelled like exhaust. She felt around, looking for the release on the locking mechanism, found it and pushed against the piece of metal, but nothing opened. If she could see…Wasn't there a light in here somewhere that activated when the trunk was open? Quick. She might not have much time.

Blood rushed in her ears; her heart pounded. *Deep, slow breaths. Don't give in to panic.*

She dragged her hands across the top of the trunk over her head. Nothing there. Where was that light? She tried to remember her own car. Should have paid attention to these things.

Think.

But focusing her brain wasn't easy, fear gripping her tighter and tighter.

Ouch. She rubbed her thumb over the pad of her index finger. What was that? She felt the roof again, carefully, and found a small piece of sharp metal—probably the end of a screw. She had to be careful with that.

Her side pulsed with pain at every move, but she kept going. The light had to be here somewhere. In the back corners, she remembered suddenly and moved her hands in that direction, hoping it would be the same in this car.

She could hear the radio up front, some twangy country music. Then a man sang. She couldn't make out the words.

Who was he and what did he want with her?

Waking up in a body bag left her less than optimistic.

The car slowed and rattled, the sounds of the road changing to that of gravel crunching under the tires. A dirt road? Where? How long had she been out?

She kept up her search of the trunk, came across some kind of lever and pulled it. Something shifted behind her. The back seat—one of those that were split in two, one side folding down for storage.

It opened only an inch or two, and she didn't dare push any farther. A narrow strip of light came through from the cab. Was the man alone? So far, she hadn't heard another voice.

Kaye held her breath, desperate for a way out. Could she make it to the inside of the car, grab the man from behind and force him to stop? That might have saved her if they were in a busy area with others around, people who could come to her aid.

The gravel crunching under the tires gave her little hope. They were out in the country somewhere. Even if she could somehow get out of the car, he would re-capture her. She was injured—she hoped to God it wasn't too bad. He had a knife. He might have other weapons as well—a gun. Maybe he had used the knife at the hospital only because it made the least noise.

She pushed the body bag down her legs and freed them. Whatever happened next, she would need as much mobility as possible. She needed a plan.

The car slowed.

She needed a plan *now*.

Pain screamed in her side as Kaye moved her arm so she could look at the dial on her watch in the narrow shaft of light that filtered through from the car to the trunk. A little after seven in the evening. She'd gone to the hospital with Cal around three, spent an hour or so waiting before she'd been tricked into that office. Her kidnapper had had a good three hours of travel time. Where were they? The vast woods of Virginia came to mind.

She had to crawl through to the car without the man noticing her somehow and gain control of the vehicle. Once she had a chance to think about it, she realized there was no other way. She had little illusion about what would happen once he reached his destination. He was going somewhere to get rid of her body.

She took a couple of deep breaths, flexed leg muscles that had gone numb. Her side felt wet and sticky; whatever wound he'd inflicted was still bleeding. The longer she waited, the weaker she was going to get.

But before she could make her move, the car rolled to a slow stop. Somebody outside was talking. The driver responded then moved on before she could decide whether or not to call for help.

They didn't go far after that. The car finally came to a halt and the motor turned off. The vehicle rocked as the man got out and slammed the door behind him.

Fear stole her breath. He was coming for her.

She listened for his footsteps. As soon as he was far enough from the driver's-side door, she'd push forward, press down the locks. If he'd left the keys in the ignition, she was as good as free. If he hadn't, she still might find his cell phone, or tumble onto the secret of hot-wiring. Looked easy enough in the movies. Pull some wires, touch them together.

But the man didn't walk toward the trunk as she'd expected. His shoes crunched on gravel, growing fainter and fainter as he walked away.

Now.

She pushed the seat forward inch by inch, ignored the pain in her side and crawled through the gap, keeping her head down. She was in the middle of the woods, in some kind of a rustic compound. Wooden huts and storage buildings loomed ahead. Nobody around that she could see.

She turned her attention to the interior. The ignition was empty.

She climbed over the seats and checked the glove compartment. No cell phone.

Okay, where were the wires?

Voices carried in the silence of the night, coming from somewhere to her left. She ducked.

"He told you not to go back, Bobby."

"Got the job done, didn't I?"

"Damn lucky. If you'd messed up now, Ben would have shot your ass off."

They were coming closer.

Kaye moved over to the passenger side, reached for the door. She slid out silently. The woods were less than twenty yards ahead.

She kept close to the ground and made a dash for it.

God, moving hurt.

She kept going. She had to get as far away from the place as she could. Find a road, a town, a phone, someone to help her.

DANNY CAUGHT UP with Congressman Brown in front of the lawyers' offices where he and some of his family had been discussing the will.

The man was tall and portly, easy to recognize from the pictures he'd seen of him. He'd thoroughly researched his files. Fifty-six, a conservative with few close friends, but considerable respect from his peers.

Why was he going up against Kaye every chance he got?

"Congressman Brown?"

Brown glanced at him, but didn't stop walking. He sent one of his security guards over to speak with Danny. He was traveling with two.

"Can I help you?" The security man was big, with a discouraging look on his face.

Danny flashed his all-purpose government ID. "I'm investigating Congresswoman Miller's disappearance. It's imperative that I talk to the congressman immediately."

The bodyguard nodded and walked back, passed on the message.

Brown hesitated for a few seconds, watching him. Then he made up his mind, said something to his family and returned with the two men.

"Daniel DuCharme," Danny said as he extended his hand. "I appreciate that you're willing to talk to me."

"What's this about Kaye Miller disappearing?"

"The congresswoman was kidnapped," Danny said, watching the man closely.

"I'm sorry to hear," Brown said without emotion and glanced toward his car. "I'm pressed for time at the moment."

"This won't take long. Perhaps we could talk somewhere private?"

Brown looked back to the car that was

waiting for him, his family still inside. "Tell the driver to take them to the hotel, then come back for me," he said to one of his security guards, then turned to Danny. "Come," he said and headed up the stairs of the lawyer's office. "Steve will let us use an empty conference room, I'm sure."

He was right. The senior partner of the firm was more than accommodating.

"I get the feeling you're not crazy about Congresswoman Miller." Danny cut right to the point as soon as they were alone.

Brown had asked his security to wait outside.

"We disagree on a number of things."

"You disagree with her more than anyone else." He pushed. "Even if you supported an issue in the past, as soon as she gets behind it, you seem to turn."

"I investigate things. Sometimes what I learn makes me change my mind about the things I supported. It has nothing to do with the congresswoman. I certainly didn't orchestrate her kidnapping."

"For the record—" Danny leaned

forward. "Where were you last Friday night between midnight and two in the morning?"

The man thought for a while. "At home in bed."

"Your wife was present?"

He shook his head. "She brought our daughter up here for the weekend to visit my mother. I was supposed to come with them, but something came up."

From the tone of his voice it seemed he regretted that decision now. Had he been too late in coming? It wasn't any of his business. Danny pushed aside the feeling of sympathy for the man. He would sympathize with him *after* he cleared him.

"Was that the night Kaye's house got broken into? I saw it on TV. It was, wasn't it? Are you implying I'm a suspect?" His gaze turned cold.

Danny shook his head. "I'm not at liberty to discuss the investigation at this stage."

"Am I a suspect?"

"There are a couple of red flags," Danny said without answering the question directly.

"Should I have my lawyer present?"

A lawyer would slow things too much.

"This is just an interview. You are not the subject of an official investigation."

Brown seemed to relax. "I don't know anything about Congresswoman Miller's troubles."

"But you're not broken up over her disappearance? As a colleague, I would have expected more concern."

"She is not one of my favorite people."

"Why?"

"For personal reasons."

They were wasting time. Danny stood. "Kaye Miller was kidnapped, and I'm going to investigate every possible angle until I find her. You can either tell me what happened between the two of you and set my mind at ease that it doesn't have to do with her kidnapping, or I will find out on my own and your personal reasons are going to become very public."

Anger flooded the man's face as he came to his feet. For a few seconds he tried to stare down Danny, then he gave up and walked to the window. "My reasons have nothing to do with this."

"I want to hear them all the same."

Brown was looking outside, his gaze fixed on something on the street. When he spoke, Danny could barely hear him. "Ian Miller had an affair with my wife."

For a moment, Danny couldn't respond. He hadn't expected that.

"When?"

"Years ago. I think it was just before he married Kaye."

"You can't possibly blame *her* for it?"

"I don't. But she's a reminder."

"Have you ever talked to her about this?"

"No. But she knows all about it, I'm sure." He ran his fingers through his hair. "I'm an old-fashioned man. I'd rather not be confronted with my wife's infidelity day after day. Every time Kaye Miller looks at me during a speech, I wonder if that's what she's thinking, if she pities me. She had obviously forgiven Ian. I could never forgive Suze."

"So you vote against the congress-woman?"

"Not consciously, no." He shook his head. "I've never really noticed, but if you say you checked the records—" He took a deep breath. "I suppose I'm not inclined to agree with her."

"But she had nothing to do with it." Kaye had said Ian and she had been dating for years before they got married. That meant she'd been just as cheated on. "How can you be angry with her?"

"She's the tragic, young, beautiful widow. Do you know the kind of votes that gets? Soon she'll become Speaker of the House. I'm nothing but a cuckolded old bastard."

Danny's phone buzzed in his pocket. He reached for it and checked the caller, then picked up immediately.

"Cole's been making phone calls. I think we've got something," the Colonel said.

"Are we done here?" Congressman Brown stood by the door.

"Yes. Thank you for your cooperation," Danny said and, as soon as the door closed behind the man, he got back to the Colonel. "Who was Cole calling?"

"The New Brotherhood."

"Damn." The hate group had been getting increasingly militant, warranting the attention of anti-domestic terrorism forces, but had not committed any acts of violence that law enforcement knew of. Looked like they had just crossed the line.

"Are you sure?" The group was conservative to the extreme, but it wasn't as if Kaye was a flaming liberal. There had to be several dozen people in Congress with voting records far more in opposition with the reclamationists than hers.

"Congressman Cole made a couple of calls after you left him. Sounds like he's been involved in this from the beginning."

"Did you trace the calls?"

"The tech team is working on it. The receiving cell is encoded pretty well."

"Have you questioned Cole?"

"He's been in surgery. They'll call me as soon as he's out."

"Where do I go for pickup?"

"To the NYPD chopper pad. I wish I could meet you at the hospital." The man's voice sounded strained. "There's an emergency meeting at the DHS. I'm not sure when I'll be getting out. I was pulling some men to help you. Can't get it done, Danny. You're it."

Whatever was going down had to be serious. Emergency meetings between the head of the SDDU and the Homeland Security Secretary happened only in response to large-scale, immediate terror threats. They were few and far between and usually required immediate relocation of resources. The SDDU had been lucky so far and had managed appropriate response in every case, heading off disaster without the American public ever finding out about it.

"Good luck, Colonel."

"Thank you, we're going to need it. And the same to you, Danny. Kaye means a lot to me. I'm trusting you with her life."

"I'm not going to let you down."

He made a run for it, and twenty minutes later, he was strapped in and flying south, just passing Philadelphia. He used the time to scroll through the security video from the small hidden camera he'd installed to cover the front of Kaye's house. There were four videos altogether, one covering each side. He had seen the recordings several times—they had been downloaded to his cell phone—but he kept thinking there had to be something he'd missed. Something that could lead him to Kaye. They had a face at least. That was a start.

The flower boy came up the path. Baggy pants, funky sneakers, walking the tough-dude walk most boys tried on at one point on their journey of growing into men. For the most, the bouquet covered his face.

One of the Secret Service agents was right behind him.

The bouquet lowered for a split second before the boy walked into the house. Two minutes and thirty-one seconds passed before the Secret Service agent rushed out shouting something. Then another minute and fifty seconds before the boy left. Not much to see there but the back of him, his baggy jeans and black T-shirt as he walked out of range of the camera that was aimed at the front stoop.

Danny swore as he scrolled back the recording frame by frame. He stopped at the point where the boy lowered the vase just as the door opened.

Who the hell are you?

The boy, seventeen or so, looked familiar, but he couldn't place him to save his life. That nose and that chin. He knew those features.

He should have been there. Damn that nosy reporter in the back. Was it possible that the man was there specifically to distract him? He'd checked out okay, but…He was about to be checked out again.

Danny closed the video file and placed a call to Sylvia.

Chapter Six

"I don't have to talk to you." Congressman Cole's face was as colorless as the pillow under his head.

"We already know you're involved." Danny stood on the right side of the bed. "Your phone calls were recorded."

A faint flush crept to the man's cheeks. "You had no right. That's illegal."

"So is attempted murder and kidnapping. If anything happens to her, you'll be an accessory to murder."

Cole closed his eyes and remained silent.

"We have the tapes. You are past the point where you could still save your career. The best you can do now is save Congresswoman Miller."

"I never meant for anything to happen to her," he said with resignation.

Okay. They were finally getting somewhere.

"Why don't you tell me where she is?"

"I don't know."

"How long have you been a member of the New Brotherhood?"

"They used to be called the reclamationists," he said in a weak voice. "I had no idea what they were about. I got recruited in college. I thought it was one of those secret societies like Skulls, at Yale University." He paused to gather strength. "I thought I'd be making contacts that would help me in the political arena I was preparing for. I figured out the truth a month or so later and never went back."

"Then why are you still in contact with them now?"

"They were blackmailing me."

"With what?"

"The membership record. My signature is in the book."

That made sense. Over the last decade, the New Brotherhood had turned into an all-purpose hate group that was becoming increasingly militant. If Cole's association with them came out, he would have been forced to resign. Which still didn't excuse his actions.

"You sold Kaye out."

"I was trying to save her life." He paused to catch his breath. "They told me to do what I could so she wasn't elected Speaker."

"And you did. Nice friend."

"They said either I stopped her, or they would. She wasn't going to make Speaker either way." He was getting agitated now. "If I couldn't keep her from the position, they would take her out permanently."

"Notifying the police didn't occur to you?" Danny bit out the words.

"At first, I didn't think they really would harm her. I was doing everything I could. It's not just my own career. Liz, my wife, is in the mayoral elections this year." He closed his eyes for a moment. "She's supported me in my career for the last twenty years. Anything that comes out about me will kill her career, too."

"But your efforts on the Hill didn't work. You knew about Kaye's accident in the tunnel. You knew the Brotherhood was getting serious. Why didn't you come forward then?"

"*I* bumped her in the tunnel." Cole lifted his head. "I did it to try to save her. I made sure she got extra security."

And it made sense suddenly. The amateurish attack in the tunnel that was so different from the semi-professional attempts later.

"You could have killed her."

"I wasn't trying to hurt her, just scare her. I wanted to make sure she would get security around the clock."

"What do you know about the men who took her?"

"Nothing. I was always contacted by phone."

"Do you know where she's being held?" The Brotherhood had compounds in several states.

"I don't know. The only man I ever talked to never told me anything. I only know his first name, and even that is probably fake. He had me call him Benito."

Benito.

Danny stood as the gears clicked in his brain. Then he took off running for the chopper that waited for him on the hospital roof. He didn't waste time calling the Colonel until they were in the air.

He wasn't back from his emergency meeting yet.

"Benjamin Mezger," Danny dictated the name to Sylvia. "The boy on the security video must be his younger brother."

Some years ago, Danny had been slated to go undercover into a rapidly growing militia group, but he'd been pulled in at the last minute and sent on an international mission. He'd recognized the boy's features because he'd spent considerable time studying the mug shots of the group's leaders.

He'd been supposed to infiltrate a subgroup in Arkansas, one that Ben Mezger had founded before moving on to Virginia. Some of Mezger's buddies had called him Benito after Mussolini, the Italian dictator.

He gave what he knew to Sylvia, and she ran the information through all the law-enforcement databases. She had a location for him within ten minutes.

"He might be out by Doher in the hills. There's a record of the cops being called by a couple of hikers who were harassed in the area a few months ago. They said they saw some kind of a camp, but the cops couldn't find it."

"How good a location do we have?"

"Not very. Want me to send a chopper to check out the area?"

"I don't want them to know we're coming. If Kaye is there, I don't want them to move her. Just have them drop me in as close as possible to where we know the camp is, and I'll find it on foot."

A compoundful of men were bound to leave plenty of tracks in the woods. He was trained for these kinds of missions.

KAYE WALKED and stumbled for only a few hundred yards before she realized she wasn't going to make it. There was nothing around her but forest, no lights beckoning from the distance. Her best chance of finding a phone was back at the compound. Her two options were going back there or bleeding to death in the woods.

She turned around and prayed she would have the strength to make it that far.

The eerie sounds of the night scared her senseless. Her love of outdoors didn't expand beyond her well-tended garden. She wasn't the outdoorsy type.

She kept on walking, stumbling through the undergrowth. The way back to the compound seemed longer. Probably because she was losing strength rapidly. At the end, she almost missed it, walking blindly through the woods. The barking of a dog and some shouting pointed her in the right direction.

The compound wasn't as quiet now as when she'd arrived. People were running around with flashlights, instructions were being yelled.

"She can't be far."

"You take the east ridge."

"She'll go toward the road."

Too bad nobody mentioned which way the road was.

Kaye kept to the shadows of the woods and surveyed the buildings, then picked the largest and crept over to it. Not all buildings had lights, but this one did. The hum of a generator betrayed the source.

She came up inch by inch and peeked through the window. The small room contained a metal bed, a chair and a desk, an old military footlocker.

Two men ran by her in the dark, just a few feet away. If everyone was looking outside, the safest place to be was inside. She wedged her fingers under the window frame and wiggled it up.

God, it hurt to be climbing.

Desperation pushed her forward. *Pull up. One leg over, then the other.* When she was in, she closed the window behind her and wiped away the bloodstains she'd left.

The table held a jumble of papers, sheets of blueprints, schedules, newspapers, garbage, a dog-eared porn magazine. No phone. She searched the footlocker next and found nothing but a few sets of worn army fatigues.

She moved to the door, opened it an inch and peeked out. A short, dark hallway—empty. She stepped from the room, keeping her ears on the noises filtering in from outside—mostly swearing and nasty jokes.

This room looked the same as the first, except for the heap of clothes by the foot of the bed. She went through the pockets. Some change, a wad of toilet paper. Bingo. Her fingers closed around a small cell phone.

But she didn't have the chance to dial. There were footsteps out in the hallway and they were coming straight toward her. She had just enough time to dive under the bed before they came in.

Four boots, two men.

"I could kill the idiot," one of them said.

"Freaking Bobby. He's always jumping the gun."

"I told him a hundred times to leave Miller alone until our priority mission was accomplished."

Another man came in.

"I'm sorry. I messed up. I thought I had the bitch."

It had to be Bobby.

One of the others shoved him. "You didn't think. You never do. Now everything is compromised."

"No way. I got her good. I thought she was dead. There was enough blood." He scraped his white sneakers across the wood-plank floor. "She won't make it far. She'll bleed out before long."

"You better hope and pray. Because we're too far gone with the plans. Things are already in motion for Friday."

What was on Friday? She tried to think of the schedule for the House. They'd be voting on a resolution to ensure fair distribution of U.S. humanitarian assistance. There were couple of other small items she couldn't quite recall.

The Senate? Nothing there, either.

The only significant political event she could think of for Friday was the Friendship Summit. The president was flying to California to meet with the president of

Mexico to discuss the new immigration reform, part of which would be a general amnesty.

Was that the target?

Compound in the woods, men running around in mismatched camouflage uniforms. Sure didn't look good. She had to get this information to Cal and she had to do it fast.

"Nothing they can do to stop us this time. This time we have it figured out," one of the men said.

"Damn right. They're not gonna see this one coming, the sons of bitches." Another spat on the floor not two feet from her face.

Who were they? Some kind of militia? A hate group? That made sense. Maybe they didn't object to her politics as much as to her heritage. And a lot of those groups were anti-immigrant as well— keep the country pure and all that.

Somebody shouted something outside. She didn't understand the words. Two of the men left, Bobby and the one who had shoved him. The third guy remained and sat on the bed.

"DUMB-ASS Bobby screws up, we get sent out here for mosquito bait." The first man pushed through the bushes.

"Damn woman ain't worth it. City girl." The second man spat. "She'll be dead good enough on her own."

"She'll have a heart attack the first spider she sees."

Danny crouched, still as the tree behind him, watching through the sparse leaves of the undergrowth, biding his time, listening to the men.

Kaye was alive, and she had escaped. He'd had a high regard for her since the beginning, but it had grown ten-fold in the last couple of hours.

When the men had passed, Danny moved through the woods like a ghost, stopping now and then when he heard others. *Come on.* Time was everything. He had to find Kaye before the men did. Trouble was, he could find no trace of her, no matter how hard he'd looked, the task made more difficult by the soldiers of the New Brotherhood traipsing all over the place, confusing the tracks.

They'd been out for hours and he with them. He didn't dare let them too far out of sight for fear that they'd find Kaye first. If that happened, he was prepared to attack at a moment's notice. But so far, the night had yielded results neither for him nor for his enemies. Maybe he would have better luck now that the moon was finally out from its cloud cover.

His cell phone vibrated once in his pocket. He made sure no one was within hearing distance, then flipped it open.

"Any news, Colonel?"

"Kaye called in. She is inside the compound, in the largest building. She's lost some blood."

But she's alive, he thought, and his heart rate steadied.

He knew the exact location, had circled the camp twice upon arrival before he'd figured out from the upheaval that they didn't have Kaye. "Anything else?" He ran without sound.

"She sounded weak. I think she said she was under a bed with people coming and going from the room. She had to hang up in mid sentence."

"I'm on my way." Danny closed the phone and doubled his speed.

He didn't slow until he was about a hundred feet from the camp.

He could only see three men, one cleaning his gun, another smoking next to the open fire, the third sleeping in a makeshift hammock. He listened, but couldn't hear voices coming from any of the cabins. The rest of the soldiers must have run off to search for Kaye.

He moved with care. The Colonel had said she was in the largest building. In the makeshift camp, that meant a ten by twenty cabin. He crept up to the back, looked through the window and caught sight of a man writing at a desk. The room was too small to have taken up the whole building. There were others, but how many? And how many men did they hide?

Impatience pumped his blood.

The man kept writing.

Blow the sucker away, grab Kaye, get the hell out of there.

That would have been the most satisfying way, but not the best. He had no backup. If he alerted the others to his presence, one could grab Kaye. Stealth was an important factor in every operation—in a solitary operation it was perhaps the most crucial element.

He rounded the building and stepped into the woods, walked a few hundred feet before he let some bullets fly into the air.

The men came in a hurry, passed right by him as he crouched in the cover of the bushes. He circled back to his target, looked inside, but couldn't see anyone. He was through the window in three seconds.

Kaye wasn't under the bed.

Where was she? He checked out the hallway, crossed to the other door. That room was dark.

"Kaye?" He whispered the single word as he stepped forward, not letting himself think that he might not find her. She was here somewhere. She had called.

"Kaye?"

In the shaft of light the open door let in, he saw something move under the bed.

He was on his knees and pulling her out the next second. "I'm here."

"I don't feel good," she said, her voice hoarse.

He looked her over as he hauled her up. She was dirty and sweaty, her hair bedraggled, her cheek scratched in a spot. She was the best damn sight he'd ever seen.

"How badly are you hurt?" He ran his hands over her arms, looking for anything broken. Her legs had to be okay—she was standing.

He saw the patch of dried blood on her side even before she pointed to it, would have gladly killed the bastard who'd done that if he could have gotten his hands on him. He hoped he'd have the honor of being on the cleanup crew that came in after Kaye was tucked away in safety.

Which was why he was here. He snapped to it and lifted Kaye into his arms. She didn't look as though she would be up to climbing and running. He glanced at the window, then thought, *to hell with that*. He wasn't going to jiggle her around and cause her more pain than he had to. To hell with stealth. He had her. His main objective now was to get her to a hospital as fast as he could. If anyone saw them he'd deal with them. His right hand, hooked under her knees, held his handgun, safety off.

"Ready?"

She nodded weakly against his chest.

"Here we go. Hang on," he said and kicked open the cabin's front door.

Camp was empty, the men still probably looking for the source of the gunfire. Danny made a beeline for the trees.

He could hear some shouting a hundred feet or so east of them. He flattened against a tree, holding Kaye tightly. When the men were out of hearing distance, he moved on.

A dog barked somewhere behind them.

What dog? He hadn't seen one before. It must have been out with one of the search teams.

"I can walk," Kaye whispered against his shirt.

"Not fast enough." He pushed harder. Even his strength and speed could turn out to be insufficient. He was running through unfamiliar terrain, while his pursuers probably knew every tree. He scrambled over a fallen log, slowed when he caught a small groan from Kaye.

"Are you okay?"

"Just a little dizzy," she said.

"Blood loss." And she was probably dehydrated, too. He stopped for a second and set her down. He took his water bottle off his belt and lifted it to her lips, happy to see that she was strong enough to hold it.

"Who are these people?" she asked once she'd slaked her thirst.

"Militant hate group. White supremacists."

She nodded soberly. "The guy who took me, the others called him Bobby. I think he was the one who came to the house, too. When we were in the attic—" Her hand fluttered up to her neck as she remembered. "He said something about me climbing too high. I thought he meant going all the way up there." She shook her head.

"Speaker of the House," he said. "Third in line for the presidency."

The noises behind him grew a little fainter. Maybe the men had gone off in the wrong direction. He hoped so. Kaye needed a moment of respite.

"Let me see your injury."

The stain on her shirt was no longer brown. The fabric was soaked red with fresh blood. He pulled the material aside, wiped the area enough so he could see what he was dealing with. The wound was shallow; the knife had probably bounced off a rib. But the cut was made in an unfortunate place in an unfortunate way so it moved every time she moved, unable to heal. He pulled out his small emergency kit and opened the tin, put it on the ground.

"You're going to sew me together?" She kept a brave face, but he caught a twinge of something in her eyes. Revulsion? Fear?

"No." He gave her a steady smile. "You'll be in a hospital in an hour. It'll hold until then." He cleaned the wound and dressed it.

"How are you?" she asked. "I wasn't sure if you could come."

"They would have to kill me to stop me." Didn't she know that?

"They came close." She passed the bottle back to him.

"Hungry?" He fished a protein bar out of his shirt pocket and handed it to her, grinned when she devoured it in two unlady-like bites.

"Sorry." She wiped her mouth. "I was starving."

"You want another?"

The way she was looking at him just then, he would have given her anything.

"Kaye?" He stepped closer and leaned forward, brushed his lips over hers on impulse. And then, of course, the second their bodies made contact, he wanted more.

"I can't. I'm sorry." She pulled back and looked away. "I can't."

"Kaye, I—"

The dog was barking again. Closer this time. Must have picked up their scent.

"We have to go."

"Let me try and walk."

"We'll go faster if you don't."

She didn't argue, but let him pick her up.

"You did good back there," he said as he started out, ignoring the sting of rejection. "Hiding where they weren't looking. The forest would have been rougher on you. It's what I would have done."

Her chapped lips stretched into a tentative smile.

He shook his head. "I didn't even think of looking for you there. I figured you'd think as a civilian and run for the hills."

"I tried. I was too weak to do it. I thought maybe I could hold out until help came."

"You did."

"Thanks for saving me again."

"You saved yourself with that call."

"I didn't get to tell Cal everything. These people are planning some kind of an attack this Friday. I think maybe during the Friendship Summit."

That was major. "Got any details?"

She shook her head.

"Derickson and Alvarez will be discussing legalizing some of the workforce that slipped through the border over the past twenty years, a conditional amnesty for illegal immigrants," he thought out loud.

"And they are proposing a new law that would make it easier for Mexicans to receive work permits to work in the United States," she added.

"Not the kind of changes The Brotherhood would appreciate." Still, taking out two presidents was one of the boldest and most nefarious plans he'd come across during his military career.

"I don't imagine they approve much of what Derickson does in general. He's the most liberal president in decades."

The men behind them were getting closer, their voices growing louder.

He had to find water to throw the dog off scent. He hadn't come across any creeks while searching for Kaye in the woods earlier. If he did now, it would be pure luck. He rushed forward, hoping for the best.

He didn't get it.

He ran into another team that was coming back toward the compound. Where the hell had they come from?

There were men behind him, the dog sounding closer and closer. There were men ahead of him, a good-sized group judging from all the noise they made. He couldn't go left, the gorge there was too steep to attempt with Kaye.

He had to leave her.

No.

Doing that went against all his instincts, but drawing the attention of the men who hunted them was the only thing he could do for her.

He clipped his phone off his belt and pressed it into her hands, bent his head to her ear. "Keep down, don't make a sound, call for help as soon as you're alone," he said, and set her down behind the thick bushes to his right. "Don't wait for me."

He looked at her one last time before he charged forward, letting some bullets fly. Return fire came at once, from both directions. He threw himself to the ground, hoping the two teams would shoot each other, but they figured out what was going on fast and after a minute or two of desperate shouting and cursing, the fight stopped abruptly.

He stayed down and waited, shot every time he saw anything move. He couldn't win, he knew that. Even if each of his shots found its aim, which was impossible in the darkness, there were more men than he had bullets.

He crawled toward the ravine, having one goal only—to lead them away from Kaye. He didn't bother to stay quiet. He wanted them to hear him, wanted them to follow instead of searching the surrounding area.

The side of the ravine was steep, but not impossible. He grabbed for roots, tested them before putting his weight on any, avoided rocks that would roll easily. Gunfire came intermittently from above. He ducked when he had to, then moved on. For a while the men seemed to hesitate about whether or not to follow him down. Dirt and gravel rolled onto his head when the first few began their descent.

His life was not as much a question of

skill as luck. He had no cover, and the men above them had plenty of bullets. His only saving grace was that the moon had slipped into hiding again, giving him at least a chance. He lowered himself, hand over hand, searching for a foothold in crevices that were slick from moss.

Then his luck ran out and pain seared through his shoulder. A bullet. He cursed as his grip loosened on the sturdy vine he used for support. Soil crumbled beneath him, leaf mold making it hard for his feet to find purchase again. And then he was going down, down, down.

Keep up the head. He made an effort to do that. Getting knocked unconscious on a stone now would be really bad. Sharp gravel tore his clothes and skin, his body getting banged against deadwood and small boulders, but with his right arm useless, he couldn't grab on to slow his descent.

An eternity passed before he reached bottom. The bullets were still coming from above, but he couldn't run. He was too beat up even to stand.

Chapter Seven

Kaye lay on her stomach in the bushes and listened to the sound of the guns, praying that none of the bullets found Danny. She couldn't move, not because of her injury—the wound had opened up again but wasn't bleeding too badly—but because two men from one of the groups had stayed behind and were now sharing a smoke not ten feet from her.

And as long as they were there, she couldn't look around for the phone she'd dropped when they first came in her direction, nearly walking over her. She'd slipped to a safe distance quietly, but wouldn't go farther than that without the phone. Until the men left, she had nothing to do but wait.

"Who the hell was that?" one of the men asked, kicking at some dead branches.

"Who knows."

"You think he's from the government?"

"They wouldn't send just one. Probably some wacko runnin' through the woods."

"Could be some hunter. Got scared, started shooting, we shot back."

"It ain't huntin' season," the second man said, closer to her now.

She held her breath. Why was he coming over?

"So what?" His buddy was still kicking up old leaves from the ground. "Who the hell cares about hunting season around these parts anyway?"

She heard a zipper going down. Close by.

"Where are you going?"

"Damn home-made beer runs right through ya."

He was standing by the tree next to her, close enough not only to hear him splash but to smell him. She stayed still, didn't take a full breath until she heard the zipper again then the sound of his footsteps as he walked away.

He stopped. "What the hell is this?"

Kaye froze. Had he seen her?

"Somebody's phone," he said after a moment.

"Pete said he was missing his. What the hell is it doing here?" The other man came closer. "I'm going back to eat something. They won't be coming up this way. Easier up at Black Bear Pass."

She barely breathed until they moved out of hearing distance. Then she sat up and felt the shirt on her side, caked with old blood, wet with new. The men had taken her phone. She was alone in the middle of the woods, injured. And Danny...

The guns had gone silent at the bottom of the ravine. Had they killed him? No, she couldn't think like that, wouldn't until she knew for sure. Pain squeezed her chest.

She had two choices: wait until dawn and see if she could spot Danny on the bottom of the ravine, or follow the men to camp and get the cell phone back somehow. Either that or another phone could bring help. There was no way she could make it out of the woods on her own.

She decided to move on instead of waiting. If those men had left Danny in the ravine, they didn't leave him alive. If he still lived, they would take him back to the compound with them.

Her side hurt enough to bring tears to her eyes. She blinked them back, told herself she was crying from the pain. She couldn't be crying for Danny. Not until she knew for sure.

The men were talking ahead of her, taking their time. She pressed a hand to her side and followed the sound of their voices. She was careful not to trip, not to make any noise at all.

By the time they reached the compound, she was dizzy with pain. Sneaking anywhere, climbing through any windows, was out of the question. She stayed in the woods, out of sight and waited.

After a while, a slow rain began to fall, not much, just enough to chill her. She burrowed against a fallen log and covered herself with leaves.

She must have dozed because she woke

to the dog barking as the men returned. They stepped from the woods into the morning light one by one. They had Danny with them. Her heart lurched.

Four men carried him, his limbs hanging listlessly, his face covered with blood. His clothes were torn beyond recognition, exposing raw flesh. She had to look down, away from the sight.

He was dead.

Her heart stopped. Tears flushed her eyes, cold pain spreading in her tightening chest.

Sweet Lord, what had they done to him?

She glanced up at the sound of shouting, saw more men run from the barracks, watched as they tossed Danny into a small wooden hut. What were they going to do with his body?

After a while, the men settled down around the fires. Somebody started breakfast. There were few jokes and little merriment despite their apparent success.

And as she looked from one to the next, she realized why. A number of them were almost as beat up as Danny, a couple nursing bullet wounds. She wondered how many were missing. Danny wouldn't have allowed himself to be taken easily.

She slunk to the right and limped around the buildings, counted them out to find the right one. She still had Pete's phone, which was under the bed that had hidden her earlier, but she couldn't make her move for it until she gathered a little strength—maybe when the men went to sleep. Until then, at least, she wanted to stay close to what was left of Danny.

"Can't get two hours of sleep together in this place, damn it." Someone was grumbling inside one of the huts. "Now I gotta go back out again or I'll be late for work." He swore long and hard. "How the hell am I supposed to explain this face to the line boss? He'll think I've been out drinking and fighting. He's been on my ass as it is."

Kaye moved on and after a while could no longer hear the guy. She found the back of the hut she'd been looking for and peeked through the slats in the wood. All of the buildings were like that, badly made with plenty of gaps. She could make out Danny's dark bulk on the ground for a while before tears flooded her eyes again and she could no longer see.

A hodgepodge of pictures flashed through her mind. When they'd first met, when he'd saved her up in her attic, when he had tried to kiss her and she'd pushed him away. She wished now that she hadn't done that. She'd pushed him away for what? For pride? For false modesty? For some misguided notion that she owed it to her image? Her career?

And now he was dead, had given his life for her.

She pulled up her knees and rested her forehead on them. Her body hurt all over, inside and out. She wanted to stay there as she was, give up, let them find her. But some well of stubbornness inside, maybe something she'd inherited from her grandfather, wouldn't let her quit.

She would get out, no matter what she had to do. She would get out and bring these people to justice.

A small sound made her look up. Her muscles stiffened as she listened. Was anyone coming? She glanced around, toward the bushes just a few feet ahead of her, came up into a crouch, ready to move.

The sound came again, a small groan from behind her—from the hut.

She pressed against the wall, desperate to see.

"Danny?"

No response.

Was his chest moving? She stared without blinking, but couldn't tell. His finger. His finger looked like it might have twitched for a second.

Could he be still alive?

The possibility loosened some of the tightness in her heart, adrenaline kicking its way through the rest of her body.

He groaned. A definite sound. Coming from him.

"Danny?" She shoved her fingers between the boards, ignoring the splinters. "I'm right here."

His body shuddered as he rolled onto his back, then looked at her—or tried. His eyes were just about swollen shut.

He said something, but she couldn't understand him. He said it again. "Go."

Before she could protest, the door banged open. She snatched her hand back. The two men who entered didn't look friendly.

The taller of the two started out by kicking Danny in the side. "Who do you work for?"

Danny didn't respond.

The man kicked him harder. "Did you have anybody with you?"

The other guy hauled him up from the ground and held him while his buddy punched him in the stomach. And when he still wouldn't talk, the man did it over and over again.

They were going to finish him off—beat him to death.

She needed a weapon. She glanced around and found nothing but small sticks. *Maybe something in camp.*

Stones and branches cut into her skin as she crawled on her stomach. About twenty men sat around the campfires, some tending their injuries.

She glanced at the nearest window. If she were to get inside one of the buildings it would have to be through the back. But not this cabin. Voices filtered from inside.

She moved back into the bushes and went around, keeping an eye on the men and the dog that was busy begging for scraps. As long as the dog didn't notice her, she was all right.

A small shovel leaned against the oak at the edge of the clearing. Would that help? Had to be better than nothing, although not nearly as good as a rifle would have been. *Watch the ground. Don't step on a branch. Keep low.*

She moved little by little until she was directly behind the tree. The only thing left to do was to reach out and grab the shovel. She waited and watched. How quickly could she grab something that was out in plain sight? What if somebody saw her?

Danny would die if she didn't help him.

Somebody swore loudly in the cabin where he was being held, then the sounds of beating resumed. A couple of people laughed around the fires, their attention momentarily diverted.

Kaye grabbed the shovel and pulled it behind the tree, then waited motionless.

Nobody raised the alarm.

She took a long breath and moved back further, into the woods. The going was slow and painful. She was careful not to disturb any bush, not to make any noise. The cabin was quiet when she got back to it.

She refused to think, simply acted. If she thought at all, she would have had to consider that the silence meant she was too late, and she couldn't accept that. She moved up to the boards inch by inch, looked through the gap.

There were two bodies on the floor, a man bent over them, collecting weapons. He moved as if he were broken. But she knew those wide shoulders. The muscles in her shoulders that had been drawn so tight they hurt, finally relaxed a little.

Danny.

"I'm here." Her whisper stopped him as he headed for the door.

He came to her and knelt on the ground, brushed his fingers over hers through the gap. "You shouldn't have come back."

She held up the shovel with her other hand. "I got this."

She couldn't tell for sure in the dark of the hut and with his face all messed up, but he might have grinned. "You were going to dig me out?" He kicked at the dirt floor, apparently considering.

"I would have done whatever I could." She hadn't gotten as far as actually making a plan. She'd taken the first tool/weapon she could find and rushed back to him.

"It could work," he said and thought for a moment. "Since you're still here, I probably shouldn't just go out there and start a war." He put the guns down. "Wedge the shovel between the boards like this."

She did as he showed her. The dried-out board gave with a quiet pop. Enough room opened up for her to pass the shovel to him and he did the rest. Once four of the boards were pushed aside, he had enough room to squeeze out sideways.

He gave her a handgun and kept the rifle. "Let's go."

She followed him into the woods, toward safety as dawn began to light up the sky. They made it. They'd gotten away. Danny was alive. She kept focused on those thoughts instead of on her side that hurt with every step. She pressed her hand to the wound and kept pace with him, step after step. Him carrying her was out of the question now; he could barely carry himself.

They were pitifully slow—both of their bodies damaged. Still, they walked a good hour before he allowed them a break.

"We can afford a few minutes." He looked her over carefully, touching her with so much tenderness, it made her throat ache. "How are you holding up?" he asked with his head cocked and those incredible eyes watching her face through swollen lids.

His skin had split over one eyebrow, both of his cheekbones and his chin. His nose was swollen and starting to turn dark. She rubbed away the tear that rolled down her cheek.

"Are you hurting a lot?" His hands—knuckles busted—came to her shoulders.

She shook her head. "What have they done to you? You were so beautiful," she said through more tears, her emotions taking over now that they were relatively safe, making her babble.

He gave a strangled laugh that made his split lip bleed. "You thought so, huh? Good to know."

He was either trying to wink or give her a cocky leer, she couldn't tell which since his face wasn't working right.

"What else? Did you think about me a lot?"

She laughed, almost giddy all of a sudden. They were finally away from camp and still alive. Near death sure put all her other worries in perspective. She wiped her tears. "Not much, really."

"Uh-hum."

"Oh, for heaven's sake. That's the trouble with handsome young guys. There's just no end to their conceit." She rolled her eyes dramatically as she limped away.

"Hey, who are you calling handsome?" He came after her.

It wasn't funny. Really. Not with his face beaten as badly as it was, but the way he said it made her smile again. And then she turned too fast, which brought on a flash of pain. She touched her hand to her side.

He was all serious the next second. "Are you in pain?"

"Not as much as you are. At least I had a little time to heal."

"Don't worry about me. I've been worse."

"Than what? Resurrected?" The only way she could picture him worse would have been if he was dead.

His swollen lips twitched.

He needed medical help. So did she.

"What's this?" She stared at the spot of fresh blood on his shoulder.

"Got nicked. Flesh wound." He shrugged it off.

"I want to put something on it before we go."

"If it makes you feel better." He ripped off the whole sleeve and handed it to her.

She did the best she could under the circumstances. "I'm sorry I lost the phone. We could go back—"

"I could go back," he said. "But there's no way I'm leaving you behind again. I'm going to get you out of here as fast as I can."

"But we have to let the Colonel know about the Summit. What if we don't get out of here in time?"

"We will." He took a deep breath and stood. "Ready?"

She wasn't. She got up anyway.

They walked another hour then rested again, this time by a creek. They stayed longer than before and took the opportunity to wash. She took care of his face as best she could and placed handfuls of leaves soaked in cold water over the worst of his injuries, hoping the makeshift poultice would take down the swelling.

She was the one now who wanted to press her lips to his, to feel them warm and alive. She couldn't. The condition he was in, she would probably have hurt him.

Little by little, they made their way toward civilization, walking as best they could, taking short breaks as frequently as they dared. By nightfall, they still hadn't reached the road.

"We're going to have to spend the night here." Danny scanned their surroundings in the twilight.

"You think the road is that far?"

"A couple of miles. Maybe as many as five."

Her legs trembled as she sat on the ground. He was right. Even if he could make it, she couldn't.

He patted his pockets. "Sorry, they took everything from me. You must be hungry."

Her empty stomach was burning with acid. She'd had two protein bars to eat in two days. "I'll be fine."

"I could scare up a few bugs."

"No thanks."

"Roots?"

"No digging. You need to rest. We won't starve until tomorrow."

He nodded. "If we were by a road, we could look for road kill. Don't look like that. I had to eat it during training. Everything tastes like chicken when you're starving. Of course, if we were by a road, we could flag a car down and have him take us to a diner."

"I vote for that."

"It's probably not a good idea to start a fire," he said. "We shouldn't need one anyway. It's warm enough."

She nodded, too tired to care.

He had her repeat one more time everything she'd heard at camp. Then the time came to settle down. They scraped together a bed of leaves. He rolled onto them first, waited for her. *Here we go.* She lay next to him, careful not to touch, and turned her back.

"If you notice any visitors, let me know," he said from behind.

"You think they still might find us?" She turned her head so she could see his face in the moonlight.

"There's always a chance for everything. But I was talking about other kinds of visitors, too. Like bears. Snakes seek out warm places at night."

"Thanks for helping me fall asleep."

He put a hand on her arm. "I don't want you to be scared, but I want you to be prepared for everything."

He was right. Better to be ready for any possibility than to be caught by surprise and panic. She turned to him fully. "Do you do this kind of thing a lot?"

"As often as necessary. I have to say, though—" His lips, barely swollen now, stretched into a smile. "You're by far the most beautiful partner I've ever had."

She was stiff with tension, expecting either the men or the local wildlife to attack them at any minute. How could he joke at a time like this? And him calling her beautiful wasn't fair, either. She could never forget the age difference between them, resented him just now for making her want to be something she wasn't.

"You shouldn't say things like that to me." She was flustered enough to pull a few inches further away.

"Why?" he asked, then his face went all serious. Too serious.

She froze. "What?" *Oh God, tell me there isn't a bear behind me.*

"I was just thinking that if you didn't like kissing me before I was all messed up, there's probably no chance of getting a good-night kiss now that I look like I went a few rounds in a blender."

"It's not that. I—" She probably shouldn't say this. "I liked kissing you."

The lopsided smile that split his face reached all the way to her heart. She couldn't seriously be thinking about this. Hadn't she been annoyed at him just a minute ago? She was pitiful. Pathetic. She had to have more sense than this.

What the hell. She leaned forward and touched her lips to his.

Oh God, now I've gone and done it, was her last coherent thought. Then she could do nothing but feel—with every heartbeat, with every pore, the incredible sweetness of the moment filling her from the inside out, like some hidden water vein, rising up, filling a drying well.

He didn't push for more. If he had, she would probably have pulled away. Instead, she brushed her mouth over his, then moved on to place gentle kisses over the bruises on his face. When they were done, a mutual unspoken agreement as if they thought with the same heart, she snuggled up against him, pressing her face against his neck, and let him hold her as tightly as he wanted.

"It's perfect," he said.

And she remembered another night a million years ago with an old boyfriend, who'd said that for a man, any encounter with a woman that didn't end in sex was considered incomplete and unsatisfactory.

She glanced up at Danny. His eyes told her all she needed to know.

"Perfect," she whispered against his skin. Because for this moment, he was. And since it was only a moment, she could allow herself to enjoy it instead of worrying about it.

She soaked up his heat and breathed him in. His strength was all around her. For the first time in years, despite the peril around them, she slept as peacefully as a child.

THE MAN stalked through the woods with determination. She was still out there somewhere. How far could she have gotten, injured like that? Not far. He had cut her good—good enough so that he'd thought she was dead. He wasn't going to make that mistake twice. Next time he would make damned sure the job was finished.

He was a hunter by nature and good at it. Once he picked his prey, he didn't stop until he succeeded. He had tracked a ten-point buck once for three weeks through the woods, living off the land. The antlers were nailed over his front door.

He would find Kaye Miller. Hunting was in his blood. He didn't know how to stop until the kill was made. And this hunt proved to be more challenging, more exciting than any he had done before. His prey was smart, but he didn't expect her to give him much more sport. He'd seen the blood at the hospital and in the body bag. If she kept moving, the wound wouldn't get the chance to close. Most likely, she was down by now, holed up somewhere, too weak from blood loss. Chances were better than good that she was already dead.

Whatever had happened to her, he had no intention of stopping until he had the body—one way or the other.

DANNY LISTENED to the voices of the night, his body aching, his blood restless. He looked at the woman in his arms, engulfed by emotions he hadn't asked for and didn't understand. He hadn't expected this. Sure, somewhere down the line when he settled down. But not now, not with this particular woman. Kaye Miller. The Colonel was going to kill him.

He didn't care.

At least she felt it, too—whatever it was they had between them—no matter how hard she tried to fight it. She hadn't realized yet that neither of them had a choice.

She was going to change his life—had changed it already simply by entering it. Kaye Miller, future Speaker of the House. God, he was going to have to go to parties and wear a tux. The thought of that hurt more than his broken ribs. Then he thought of her in that black dress she'd worn at The Hotel George, and smiled. Maybe going to fancy parties with her wouldn't be such a chore after all.

He would probably have to get some civilian occupation for cover. He let his mind try on a few possibilities. Security consulting? He'd be good at that. Or maybe he could open his own landscaping supply business. It would save a lot of money around the house. He enjoyed spending time outdoors anyway.

He heard a small noise in the bushes in the distance and reached for the rifle.

Whatever it was, it moved on in no particular hurry. Probably a deer. He relaxed.

Kaye stirred in his arms, so he held still, not wanting to wake her. She opened her eyes anyway, looked at him for a few seconds before she came fully awake.

"What time is it?"

"A little after three. You can rest some more."

She closed her eyelids, but they popped open again a moment later. "I didn't even ask you. How did you find me?"

"Congressman Cole is in with the Brotherhood."

"Roger?"

The pain of betrayal on her face made him want to gather her to him, but he wasn't sure how she would react to that, to some other news he still had to give her, so he stayed away.

"For what it's worth, he didn't want you to get hurt. They were blackmailing him." He told her what he'd found out from Cole.

"Roger rammed me in the tunnel? But it wasn't his car. I know his car."

"It was an out-of-state rental he happened to have that week. He saw an opportunity and took it. He wanted to do something to put your security on high alert." He filled her in on the rest, watched her face change from disbelief to anger as she processed it all.

"What's going to happen to him?" she asked when he was done with the story. "Why didn't he tell me?"

"He was scared, Kaye, that's all. When people get scared they do stupid things."

She nodded and fell silent for a while.

"I can't believe you interrogated a congressman."

"Not just one."

He really didn't want to talk about Brown, but he had to tell her at some point. Might as well get it over with. Man, but he hated to see her hurt.

"There's something Brown told me."

"He can't be in this, too." Her eyes were wide and vulnerable.

"Not in this. It's personal. It's about Ian and it might—" What the hell was he supposed to say? "It might change your memory of him. You might not want to know."

And he sure didn't want to be the one to tell her. He was interested in her, wanted her. Trashing her dead husband's memory was the nastiest thing he could imagine doing.

He watched her take a deep breath and gather new strength.

"I want to know," she said.

"He, um…He and Suze Cole, Congressman Brown's wife. I'm sorry."

"They dated in college. I knew that."

He really didn't want to say anything more.

"After we were married?" she asked after a while with a catch in her voice.

"No, of course, not. But after…after *they* were married."

"Ian would never…" She fell silent and closed her eyes.

So his instincts had been correct and she hadn't known.

"Maybe he didn't," he rushed to say. "What the hell does Brown know? Maybe he's a jealous jackass." Why the hell did he have to go and tell her? What was he, stupid? "I'm sorry. I shouldn't have said anything. It's—"

"It's okay. I'd rather know," she said as she turned her back to him. Her voice sounded off.

Was she crying?

"Kaye?"

He reached for her, but changed his mind and pulled his hand back. He had no right to touch her, no right to offer her comfort, especially since he was the one who'd made her this upset.

"Let's go to sleep," she said.

"You can hit me, or something. If it'd make you feel better."

"It's okay. Really."

He stared at the silhouette of her slim back, wanting more than anything to draw her into his arms. It bothered him more than all his wounds that he couldn't.

Chapter Eight

"Here it comes."

Kaye pulled her head down, hiding behind the bushes while Danny stood by the side of the road and waved at the dark-green pickup. The vehicle slowed, and she registered the two men inside, the gun rack in the back window—nothing to be alarmed by in this part of the state, plenty of hunters.

When they got close enough, she looked over their faces, but didn't recognize either man. Were they part of the Brotherhood? There had been too many to remember them all. She'd seen only a few, but had heard many while she'd been hiding under the bed, would recognize a number of voices.

Danny stood relaxed, probably wanting to look as friendly as he could. His face was bad enough.

She had tried to convince him to let her stand out there, but he wouldn't let her anywhere near the road.

"I need some help," he said now, making sure his hands were in plain view so they could see he was unarmed.

Then the door opened and the men got out, both with handguns pointed at him.

Kaye gripped the rifle. They were too close to Danny. She was a terrible shooter even at paintball—the only time she'd had a gun in her hands before, at Sadie's insistence. Could she risk a shot now?

"Looks like this is the end of the road for you," the taller of the two said to Danny while the other sneered.

They both wore a hodgepodge of clothing that included a few pieces of camouflage and boots. They looked fine otherwise, no sign of injury. Apparently, they hadn't been among the ones who'd tangled with Danny in the ravine.

She kept her finger on the trigger, ready,

and watched as Danny stepped closer to them slowly, his hands rising at his sides as if in capitulation. The next second he was grabbing for the handgun tucked into his waistband behind his back.

Two shots were all it took. He had the men disarmed and clutching their injuries on the ground within seconds. And she was flying out of the woods with the rifle.

"Didn't I say not to come out until I tell you?" He shook his head, but was too busy tying the men up with their belts to give her a lecture.

"Damn, him and the politician bitch were together. Do you believe this?" the short stocky guy said as he stared at Kaye.

The other one grunted with frustration as he fought against his bindings in vain. "You're gonna regret this. You don't know who you're messing with."

"A bunch of gutless losers," Danny said, and pulled the belt tight.

"Are we leaving them?" She was shaking but kept the rifle pointed at the one Danny was working on. She was close enough now not to miss, not to put

Danny's life in danger if she had to shoot. She flinched when the man let loose a string of colorful curses.

"Can't leave them." Danny tied off the belt. "Their buddies will be along soon enough, I'm sure. Anyway, Secret Service would want them for questioning."

The guy spat at Danny but missed, listed a variety of heated threats then swore some more.

"Shouldn't talk like that in front of a lady." Danny took the guy's camouflage baseball hat and gagged him with it, then did the same with the other one.

He picked up the tall man first, bit back a groan as the man jerked around in protest, but dumped him into the back of the truck. Kaye stepped forward to help with the second man.

"Don't do it. It'll open up your wound again."

"You have worse injuries."

"I'm used to working injured. You keep the gun on them. We shouldn't both lay down weapons at the same time." He glanced at the woods.

He was right. There were still others out there, looking for them.

She waited for him to finish, her rifle at the ready.

"Congressman Kaye Miller, commando babe." He grinned when they were done and sitting in the cab.

"Think I can use that in my next campaign?" Her lips twitched. They had a car. They'd made it.

"Color flyers. Nobody could resist this." He gestured at her.

She shook her head, trying not to think what her colleagues would say if they could see her now. Kaye Miller, anti-violence poster girl. Funny how life worked out sometimes.

"Let's get going," she said, aware that they were both keeping the mood light for each other's sake. They were both in bad shape, Danny worse than she. She'd be surprised if he didn't have internal injuries.

They reached a roadside gas station in half an hour and called in their location to Cal, along with what information they had on the Summit.

The chopper took less than twenty minutes to get there with a medic who started an IV on both of them the second they were inside the bird.

"Feeling better?" Danny asked.

She nodded. "Thank you." The words were woefully inadequate. What he'd done for her, that he had come for her alone...

"And thank you, Congresswoman."

She hated that he'd switched back to formality, but understood that he was doing it for her sake. She fisted her hand so she wouldn't reach out and take his. Anything beyond their professional relationship was impossible between them. Now that they were no longer alone, it was easier to remember that. Easier to remember, but not any easier to accept.

"Could you lie back, sir?" One of the paramedics was examining his face, a purplish mess crisscrossed with red lines where his skin had split during the beatings.

"How bad is it?" She couldn't help asking.

"Not bad for armed conflict, Congresswoman," the paramedic responded with a polite smile.

She took a deep breath, then another, watched the woman wash the injuries and dress them.

"Shouldn't they be stitched?"

"At the hospital. That's more careful work than we can do in the chopper." The woman worked efficiently, moving from one spot to the next.

With not much to do until they got to D.C., Kaye watched them, grabbing on to the gurney when the chopper banked to the left.

He turned to her on reflex to see if she was okay, making her smile. He smiled back.

"Are you okay?"

From the way he was looking at her, she knew he was asking about more than her physical wellbeing. They had talked little all morning, tired from hiking through the woods, feeling awkward after the conversation they'd had in the middle of the night.

"Fine. Thank you for telling me everything."

She wasn't glad for what had happened between Ian and Suze, but she would rather know it than be protected from the truth as Cal might have done. She appreciated Danny's vote of confidence that she could deal with it. In the treacherous world of politics, if Congressman Brown had something personal against her that affected their professional relationship, it was better to know so she could be on her guard.

Ian and Suze. When? She'd asked herself this a hundred times during the night. Then she'd figured it out. It had to be the summer she'd gone to Europe. She'd loved it, had told Ian she might not come back. They'd been kids.

It hurt, of course. It brought into question the Ian she knew. For a while last night, she had raged, felt fooled, felt betrayed. Then she'd realized that Ian was entitled to his own mistakes. He had made some, but he'd grown somehow through them, learning from them, into the wonderful man she had fallen in love with. Nothing could change that.

They'd had a good marriage, one that was rare by today's standards. She had loved and been loved in return. That was as big a blessing as anyone could hope for in this life.

She watched Danny watching her. And what of him? There was something there. Something warm and safe and wonderful she wanted to fall in to and be enveloped by. And it made her feel nervous. The impulse was unexpected and completely inappropriate.

Even beyond the fact that he was her bodyguard, she couldn't fall for Danny. She couldn't fall in love with him, because if she did, then what of her love for Ian? What of the idea of a once-in-a-lifetime sweeping love, the memory of which was supposed to be enough to keep her alive? It couldn't be right, to feel like that again, to feel it with another man.

She wouldn't do it. She was certainly mature and strong enough to stop now; there was still time. She turned away from Danny and looked out the window instead, just in time to see five Apache helicopters swooping in, moving in the direction of the camp.

"I CAN'T BELIEVE they're not keeping you for observation." Danny glanced back at Walter Reed Hospital, from which they had both just been released. He was fine with his treatment, but nowhere near happy with Kaye's. He should go back and talk to the doctor one more time. The woman had been stabbed, for heaven's sake. There had to be more they could do for her than slapping on some bandages. "I can't believe that doctor is letting you go."

"I can't believe you're not letting me go home." Kaye looked between the Colonel and Danny as they escorted her to the waiting black SUV. "They've done everything they could possibly do to me. I got disinfected and stitched and X-rayed and ultrasounded and labworked to death. I got a shot!" She glared at Danny.

Damn right she did. He'd made sure. In

the SDDU tetanus shots were routinely administered on schedule. Kaye on the other hand, hadn't had one since college.

The Colonel nodded to the guards who stood by his car and who had now started to stop traffic for them. "Just be glad I'm not sending you to a safe house," he said to Kaye.

Danny opened the door for her, closed it when she was in, then went around to the front passenger seat. He hated the passenger seat. Unfortunately, when the Colonel was in a car, the man was driving. He'd learned that on the way over and thought it unfair to the extreme that the Colonel would pull rank over something like this.

"The only reason I'm not at a safe house is because you think your place is safer." Kaye sulked in the back as the Colonel pulled away.

"Damn right it is."

They bickered like family. It left Danny slightly uncomfortable, feeling like the outsider. Seeing the Colonel from this angle was odd, too. At the SDDU nobody talked back to the man.

They were going to the Colonel's lair. He tried to picture it, but couldn't. When he'd agreed to this mission, he sure hadn't thought it would involve moving in with his superior officer. But there was no way in hell he would let Kaye out of his sight until everything was resolved. He would protect her any way he could, and hope his mad attraction for the Colonel's one and only goddaughter would escape the man's eagle eyes.

Boy, he was treading on dangerous ground here.

Landmine training came to mind. That's what this was going be like. One wrong move and he was likely to get his head blown off.

At least the ride to Fort Rock, as he named the place the second they drove through the security gates, didn't take long, no more than forty-five minutes. The Colonel lived just outside the city. The property, five acres or so, was surrounded by a ten-foot-high stone wall. A long driveway wound its way to the house, a cross between an old mansion and a prison.

"A retired insane asylum. I've been working on it for a couple of years," the Colonel said by way of an explanation. "The back windows still have bars on them. It's a lot of work."

And too weird by half. Danny stared. He had to be the first from the SDDU to see this place. Word would have gotten around.

The car pulled to a stop by the front steps.

Kaye was out before he could open the door for her.

He followed them up the stairs, took in the state-of-the-art security cameras that looked out of place on the old building.

The Colonel stepped up to the door, slid aside a metal plate and looked straight ahead. "Retina recognition. I'll enter you into the system later. Kaye is already in it."

"I take it you bring work home sometimes?"

The Colonel grinned. "Now and then. I try not to make a habit of it."

"I don't suppose you'll tell me now what it is exactly that you do instead of enjoying retirement?" Kaye was asking.

"Light consulting on occasion. Nothing terribly exciting."

"I bet," she said.

So Kaye didn't know, Danny thought as he followed them. He would have been surprised if she did. The confidentiality rule extended to family members—safer that way both for the family and the SDDU. Their missions had too much at stake.

He looked around the long hallway, up at the ceiling, at least twelve feet high. Kaye walked forward without looking at much, obviously used to the place. She made no further remarks on the Colonel's mysterious retirement. She worked in politics, she probably knew how things like this worked.

Outside of the hundred and twenty or so Special Designation Defense Unit members, only a handful of people knew about the existence of the group—the Secretary of Homeland Security, and a few higher-ups at the FBI and CIA who were sometimes called in when the SDDU needed those connections.

A phone was ringing somewhere.

"Would you mind showing Danny around, Kaye? He can have the room next to yours." The Colonel took off without waiting for an answer.

"Follow me." She moved forward and pointed at another metal door. "That leads to the lower level. It's better not to go there."

He could only imagine.

"This used to be the lobby. Now it's the living room."

The place was about thirty by thirty, large black-and-white tiles covering the floor. About a third of the space was taken up by an antique rug and three leather sofas, a giant entertainment center. Another corner of the room held a wet bar, surrounded by wall-to-wall bookcases.

He hadn't figured the Colonel for a bookworm.

In another spot with plenty of elbow room, a gorgeous nine-foot, rosewood pool table stretched under special lights, the Diamond Professional. Now that was more like it. He slowed and took in the view. Fine. Fine. Fine.

Kaye cleared her throat, and when he looked at her, he found an indulgent smile on her face.

"Sorry."

"It's okay. I understand," she said. "I lust after his gardens."

If they were talking about lust, he could have listed a few things—all of which included her—that he wanted considerably more than a game of pool. But he kept his list to himself as he followed her across the floor.

"Kitchen is that way." She pointed down another hallway as she moved forward on those long legs now wrapped in a pair of brand-new blue jeans the Colonel had brought to the hospital with him along with some other clothes. They made her look a lot less congresswomanish and a lot more approachable.

He tried to focus on what she was saying.

"For now, only the front part of the building is renovated. The rest is still pretty spooky. Cal had some rooms set up right here." She nodded toward a row of doors. "This is his. This one is mine. And this will be yours, if that's okay." She opened the door.

He paused before stepping inside. "Do you stay here a lot?"

"Hardly ever."

"I wonder why," he said, deadpan.

She smiled. "I love Cal, but...Why would anyone want to live someplace like this?"

Maybe because it was as impenetrable as a fort. The place was built for security to start with. By the time the Colonel finished adding in the most modern electronic gadgets, the boys at Langley probably weren't safer than this.

He stepped into the room after her, expecting a cell-like space, an old patient's room, but found instead something that looked like a spacious hotel room, equipped with the latest and best conveniences.

"Cal hired a designer," Kaye said. "These couple of rooms used to be the offices for the bigwigs who ran the place."

He looked around and out the window

to the well-kept grounds, noticed where the iron bars had been sawed off. Charming.

"I'll leave you to settle in," she said and walked out the door.

He tossed his duffel bag on the floor and looked around again, more thoroughly this time. The place was solid. How long would the Colonel want to keep Kaye here? Now that he'd seen the place, he was in full agreement with the man. This was where Kaye needed to be until all threat was over.

He hopped into the shower then put on some clean clothes. He could hear water running on the other side of the wall. Employing all his self-mastery, he didn't try to picture Kaye naked. Okay. Maybe a little.

He waited a good twenty minutes after the water stopped before walking over and knocking on her door.

"Come in."

Man, she looked good. She always did. She had class, heart, courage. Then there were those legs…

"Want to go look for the Colonel?" he asked, to remind himself where they were.

"Sure. Just give me a minute." She pulled her hair into a ponytail and twisted a rubber band around it.

She was standing at an angle in front of the wall mirror, her breasts straining against the simple T-shirt she'd put on. Nineteenth-century poets would have written sonnets about her curves. Having little literary inclination, all he could do was drool.

Or do something about it, damn it.

Before he could think too much, he moved up behind her. Their eyes met in the mirror, and he saw hers darken for a second. The next moment his hands were spanning her waist.

Then the alarm in his brain went off. He was groping Majority Whip Kaye Miller, future Speaker of the House of Representatives—in the Colonel's house. He was her bodyguard, damn it.

He slid his hands up and had her in a restrictive hold before she could blink, careful not to put any pressure on her side.

"You can't let your guard down. Not ever. Not anywhere," he said, feeling like an ass, hoping she didn't realize that his hands on her had little to do with the desire to teach her self-defense.

She twisted, lifted her arms like the handle of a corkscrew, dropped to the floor and rolled, giving a good kick to his knee at the same time.

She caught him by surprise with that. He'd been too focused on how the side of her breast felt against his chest as she slid down against him. He rubbed his knee. Served him right.

"I wish you would give me warning when you want to practice."

"Did the man who knifed you at the hospital give you any warning?" He tried to sound reasonable to keep up the charade.

She looked away, then back. "Fine. Point taken."

Her scent was still in his nostrils.

For a split second he thought he saw something in her eyes that looked a lot like the hot flash of desire that was singing through his own body.

Rules be damned.

"Do you want a warning, Kaye?" He

stepped closer. "Here's one. I'm going to kiss you."

Her eyes widened, but she didn't move away.

He bent his head, leaned his forehead against hers and for a moment just breathed her in.

He had to be insane to be doing this.

Appropriate for the location, he thought wryly before brushing his lips gently over the silky curve of her cheek.

He didn't dare put his arms around her, didn't want to push her too far.

When she closed her eyes, he kissed each eyelid in turn, then the tip of her nose.

"You have a very sexy nose, Congresswoman."

"Nobody has a sexy nose." Her lips stretched into a smile.

"You do. I noticed it a long time ago. It even comes through on TV."

She opened her eyes and looked into his. "You got a nose fetish or something, Mr. DuCharme?"

Her voice, all throaty-sounding, sent his blood rushing.

"It's not just the nose." He moved on to her chin and nibbled his way up to her ear. "There is all kinds of sexy going on here. Killer legs," he added as an example when she drew up an ebony eyebrow.

He brushed his lips across hers, then pulled back.

That was all he'd intended to do.

Hell, he hadn't even intended that. He'd intended to come and collect her then go find the Colonel and figure out what they were doing next.

But now that he'd come this far, he had trouble stopping.

Especially since she looked like she maybe, just maybe, didn't want him to stop.

"Kaye?"

She lifted her arms and placed them gently on his shoulders.

And that was the end of him.

She tasted like the happiest of his dreams, a taste he barely remembered, since he tended not to dream at all or else about the blood of old missions.

To hell with who she was. He wanted

her and he wanted her to know it. He wanted her to take him seriously this time.

And he wanted to take her as he would have taken any other woman, to prove to her that he could and, more importantly, to prove to himself that she wasn't any different, no more worthy of the strange awe and sickening puppydog-like admiration he couldn't help every time she was within sight.

He wanted to prove that the mind-bending fear he'd felt when she'd gone missing had not been real. That he hadn't panicked. He was the toughest of tough guys, super-secret special commando soldier. He needed to prove to himself that he couldn't be done in by a woman.

Somewhere in the back of his mind, twenty seconds into the kiss, he began to understand that proving anything like that wasn't going to happen.

She felt like everything and nothing. Everything he'd fantasized about kissing during his preteen years, and nothing like the experiences he'd actually ended up having since.

She shook him. He didn't like that, saw it as a sign of weakness. But he didn't want to stop. He wanted to taste her again. His brain refused to hold any thought beyond that.

His body moved with practiced ease, almost without conscious thought on his part, and steered her toward the bed. She weighed nothing. He laid her down gently, like a feather falling. She might not even have noticed it.

His hand found the spot where her T-shirt and jeans met and slipped inside. Then he stopped, his palm against her naked skin, and soaked up her heat.

Touching her like that felt like a dream, and he was afraid if he stopped, if he spoke, if he did anything at all other than what he was doing, he would wake up and never find his way back to this place again.

He kissed her as if he wanted to drink her in, to keep her inside him, keep her safe.

He let go of her lips for a moment to cover the sweet arch of her neck with his mouth.

"Danny," she said.

She didn't say it in a good way.

He moved back up to her lips quickly to stop her from saying more, to stop her from thinking, but it was too late. She was already pushing him away.

She got up fast, straightened her clothes on the way to the door.

"It's not right," she said without looking at him. "We can't do this again."

And then she walked out, leaving him flat on his back in her bed, with an empty hole in the middle of his chest.

"Wow."

Had he just said, *Wow?* Damn. Danny clamped his mouth shut. He didn't use the word often, but the Colonel's underground command center warranted it.

"It's a war room." He took in the computerized maps in the middle. Rows and rows of computer screens lined one full wall.

"What's this for? In case anyone takes the Pentagon out? Looks like you could run the country from here."

"Not the whole country." The Colonel shrugged modestly. "But it's useful to have around. All lines are one-hundred-percent secure. In case we ever suspected a leak somewhere, this could come in handy. Very few people know about it."

"So what do you do here?"

"Keep unauthorized surveillance records among other things. Every report that comes into my office gets copied to here as a backup. This pretty little thing—" He tapped the top of a computer affectionately. "Runs some mighty fancy logistics. It'll pick up on things the human mind would never connect."

"Kaye ever been down here?"

"Not beyond the dungeons. I showed her that and she hasn't shown any inclination since for a return trip."

Danny nodded. He couldn't blame her. The "dungeons," underground treatment rooms that looked more like torture chambers, were the first things to greet anyone who entered the subterranean level of the building. Dirty and dark with flickering lights and scary-looking equipment, water dripping from rusty pipes. All of it was original according to the Colonel, being used now as a clever disguise for the hidden door that opened to his personal war room.

The man pushed a couple of buttons and a report scrolled onto one of the nearby screens. Dates and events.

"Surveillance on Congressman Brown."

"You can probably stop that," Danny said, still uncomfortable with the topic. "I had a talk with him."

"You interrogated another esteemed member of Congress?"

"I needed to know what I needed to know."

"If I'm going to have to take heat over this—"

"You won't."

The Colonel dropped into a leather chair and motioned for him to do the same. "Was he in with the Brotherhood, too?"

"No. His business was all personal."

"What personal business does he have with my goddaughter? Am I going to have to go over and pay him a visit?" His voice was hard and so was his face.

A good reminder that he was not a man

to cross, and that he was fiercely protective of Kaye.

Danny drew a deep breath and told him the highlights of the story.

The Colonel had that hard look about him again by the time the tale was done. "You told her?"

He nodded.

"She had a right to know," the Colonel said after a while. "But it's probably the last thing she needed to hear right now."

Something beeped and the Colonel stood, went over to another terminal and punched up another set of reports. "Whatever is going on between the two of you, I don't want her to come out of it hurt," he said over his shoulder.

Oh, hell. Here it came. Danny opened his mouth, but the Colonel caught him off with a hand gesture.

"See that wall of monitors? Every square inch of this building is covered by pinpoint cameras. They're set on motion sensors."

"The guest rooms?" His voice came out embarrassingly weak.

"Everything."

Oh, man. The Colonel had seen him grope his goddaughter. Maybe he hadn't brought him to the "dungeons" just to show him the war room. The place seemed a lot more sinister all of a sudden. Some of the nasty machinery they'd passed on the way in popped into his mind.

"I…care for her." Had he said that?

The Colonel turned. "You think?"

"I know."

"If you hurt her in any way—"

"I won't."

The man turned back to the console. "I'm sending you two to California tomorrow. You've both seen several men from the Brotherhood. Between the two of you, you might be able to ID someone."

Danny nodded, having expected something like this. The choppers the Colonel had sent in after Kaye and he were rescued had cleaned up the camp, but at least a dozen of the men were missing, had disappeared into the woods without a trace.

"I could go alone." He had quite a few faces etched into his memory.

"She wants to go."

He understood perfectly. And since her going meant they'd be together for another day or two, he didn't fight the idea. She'd be safe enough at the Secret Service command center.

"You'll be working with the president's detail, watching from a safe location through video feed," the Colonel said, confirming Danny's expectations.

"I guess the president is not canceling the Summit."

"This president?" The Colonel glanced back and gave him a look.

"Right." President Derickson was one tough son of a bitch who didn't back down from anyone. He wouldn't alter his schedule based on a terrorist threat. He would expect his people to handle it. "That's what the Secret Service is for." He nodded.

From what he knew, Derickson got death threats almost on a daily basis— plenty of nutcases out there who got off by calling in. All were investigated; anything that proved to be a real threat was taken care of. Little of it was allowed to influence the president's schedule.

"When are we leaving?" He glanced at a printer that had started up all by itself and was now spitting out some kind of report.

"First thing in the morning. Oh-six-hundred hours." The Colonel glanced at the first page of the report, then looked up. "You bring her back to me safe."

He pinned Danny with a gaze that was as serious as he'd ever seen the man. "I won't be around," he added. "Kaye thinks I'm going to a golf resort in England with some old friends, but…There's a situation. The Homeland Security Secretary asked that I lead the team personally. Things are bad."

They had to be, Danny thought. The whole world had to be on the brink of disaster for the Colonel to leave Kaye at a time like this. He'd seen them together enough now to know that. And he would have lied if he said it didn't feel good that the Colonel would entrust her safety to him.

He would not fail either of them.

Chapter Nine

Kaye lay in bed and listened to the noises of the night. Considering the age of the place, it was surprisingly silent. The walls were made of stone, the floors all tiled, none of the creaking of wood floors and wood houses. Only the odd water pipe gurgled now and then, and the radiators rattled on occasion.

On the whole, the night was peaceful.

She wasn't.

Tomorrow she was going to try to stop a domestic terrorist attack on two presidents. The idea seemed insane.

She got up and walked over to the window, looked out at the moonlit garden, at the giant oaks bathed in silver. Too much was happening all at once. If she was elected to be Speaker should she accept it? Would it make her a target for the rest of her life? Cal would have been a good person to talk everything over with, but she was wishing for Danny's company.

He was probably asleep. She couldn't just waltz into his room this time of the night. She moved toward her bed, but then changed her mind and ended up in the bathroom instead.

They'd had a fun evening—incredibly normal. An excellent dinner followed by a few rounds of pool, which she'd lost miserably. Cal had entertained them with some anecdotes from his early years. They had laughed. Both men were as relaxed as she'd ever seen them, and even though she knew they were probably putting it all on for her benefit—she had noticed the hour they'd disappeared into the basement— she had forgotten about everything else for a while.

But the night was at its darkest now, the time when the darkest of thoughts came out, too. And all of a sudden she was unsure and maybe even a little scared. This went beyond what she'd had to face daily on the Hill. This was no policy drafting, no ideas on paper to be discussed. Lives were at stake, important lives, and she was in the middle of it all.

She tapped on the wall that separated her from Danny's room, waited, then tapped again.

He was coming through her door before she made it out of the bathroom.

He closed the door behind him. "Did you need me?"

That was a loaded question. She watched as he looked around in the room, alert, then little by little relaxed and tucked his gun behind his back. He didn't have a shirt on, his jeans were zipped but unbuttoned.

Moonlight washed over his chest and face, looking a hundred percent better thanks to the expert care at Walter Reed.

She stayed silent, unable to tell him what she wanted. Ridiculous—a Speaker who couldn't talk. She wanted him to know what she needed without her having to say anything.

And he did.

He came closer and wrapped his arms around her without any ceremony.

Yes. This was it. They didn't need to talk. Just having his arms around her, having that comfort was enough. They had been through rough times before. They'd made it out of the camp, out of the woods together. She just had to remember that.

She sank against him, a little embarrassed by her weakness, but comfortable enough with him not to care.

His lips, warm and soft, found hers in a kiss that was sweet and incredibly arousing. She opened for him, gratified by his obvious need—nice to be wanted like that, with so much passion.

She didn't think; she simply felt. It had been a long time since she'd done that. She hadn't realized until just now how much she could still need. She needed this moment, needed this man.

When he pulled away, abruptly, she almost fell after him. She caught herself at the same time as his hands came to her shoulders.

"Danny?"

He was looking up, running his gaze along the seam where the ceiling met the wall. "Maybe we shouldn't be doing this."

Okay, that was embarrassing. He couldn't even look at her.

All this time he'd done everything possible to show and tell her how much he wanted her, and now, when her resolve cracked, he looked ready to run. Maybe it wasn't her he'd wanted after all, but the chase, the knowledge that he could have her.

Disappointment rose in her throat. She turned away.

"Kaye." His hands slid to her back and stayed there. "It's just that the Colonel—"

She turned back to him slowly. "Did Cal talk to you about me?"

He didn't say anything.

Oh, God. "I'm going to kill him. I can't believe he did this." She brought her hands up to her face. "Tell me he didn't ask you what your intentions were."

He grinned.

"I'm going to— What am I, eighteen?"

"He loves you."

"He loves to embarrass me. He treats me like I'm a kid."

She moved closer to him, looked him in the eye. "I'm a grown woman, Danny. I don't need his protection and I don't need yours. Not from this. This is what I want."

He closed his eyes for a second, his dark, thick eyelashes settling on his tanned cheek. Then he opened them and she reeled from the naked desire in his gaze. "We can't. The security cameras—" He took a breath as if it hurt.

"There are no cameras here. Did he tell you there were? I *am* going to kill him." She went to the window. "There are cameras all around, but none inside this room. We had a talk about that years ago."

"No cameras?"

The eager hope on his face made her smile.

"None."

He walked to the door, slowly, deliberately, and turned the lock. By the time he came back, he was grinning from ear to ear, obviously having slipped back to the light mood they'd shared downstairs earlier in the evening.

"Honorable Congresswoman, I move to reconvene the session," he said.

"Motion accepted." She slipped into his arms.

He could kiss. Goodness, the man could kiss.

She felt as she had at fourteen, making out for the first time with the neighbor boy in her father's toolshed.

Naughty.

Except she was almost thirty-six now. The opposite of naughty. She was a grown-up, a conservative politician, a congresswoman.

She tried not to think of that as her hands sneaked up Danny's chest.

He felt good—hard muscles under soft skin with silky soft springy hair here and there—warm, steady. He was strong. A lot of other women she knew in politics were attracted to power. She wasn't. But she was a sucker for strength. The kind of unassuming, inherent strength Danny seemed to have in spades. Combined with his humor and playfulness, it made him irresistible.

She wanted to ask him to her bed and felt shy all of a sudden. She had never asked a man to make love to her before.

She pulled back just enough to be able to look him in the eye. "I want you," she said, and held her breath.

A new grin split his face. "How much?"

"Well, if you're going to play hard to get..." She raised an eyebrow.

"Can't possibly want me half as much as I want you," he said as he picked her up and carried her to the bed.

They bounced, both impatient, and groaned together. He pinned her under him and trailed kisses all over her face, full of enthusiasm and playfulness. His mood was contagious.

"You're so—" She searched for the word.

"What?"

She wasn't sure how to finish. Everything a woman could secretly desire? How pathetic did that sound? And just because he looked so cocky with that big grin on his face, so sure of himself, she said, "Cute," just to get to him.

His face turned serious. "I'm not. Take it back." He rubbed his hardness between her legs, teasing her.

For a second, she couldn't breathe, much less talk. Her body responded to the friction. The electricity between them was dizzying.

She took a deep breath. "Okay, what do you want to be called?"

"Umm." He caught her lower lip between his teeth, then let it go. "I'd prefer it if you thought of me as sexy in a very macho kind of way."

She smiled. "Yes, Mr. Stud Muffin, sir."

"That does it."

In one smooth move, he pulled her pajama top up and ran his hot, wet tongue over the valley of her breasts. The air caught in her throat again, then released as tingles skittered across her skin.

He held her in place, allowing no movement beyond a harmless squirm, and bent his head, closed his teeth over a nipple.

"Oh," she said weakly.

"You call that cute?" He murmured the challenge against her body.

No, definitely not cute. She arched her

back to press against him. He sucked hard, and she felt the V of her thighs grow wet.

He let go and blew some air on her breast. "How is this for cute?" He closed his teeth over the base of the nipple while flicking his tongue over the tip.

He wasn't cute. He was merciless.

He let go of her hands to explore the other breast then the rest of her body. He was no longer holding her down, but it was too late. She had lost the ability to move.

It wasn't fair. She was out of practice. She had forgotten—

His fingers found the waistband of her shorts.

Okay. Move. She had to do something. She couldn't lay there like a stupid doll.

She tried to gather her scattering thoughts. Focus. Hands to his shoulders. She wanted to touch him, to feel him. But then his finger dipped inside her and all she could do was to hang on to him.

"I wanted you from the second I saw you at that awards gala."

She remembered him watching her from across the room.

At the time she had felt threatened by his apparent strength. Now she was comforted and aroused by it. He was squarely on top of her, but she didn't feel smothered. She felt sheltered in his arms, safe enough to be playful.

She ran a few tentative fingers up his side.

"I'm not ticklish," he said, a tad too bland-faced.

"Oh really?" She slid her fingers higher up.

He twitched. His lips trembled slightly.

"Not even if I do this?" She circled the spot.

He bit back a laugh and flipped them so she was sprawled on top. "Okay. You found my weakness. You win. Do with me as you must."

He threw his arms and legs wide, offering himself to her without defenses.

It had the odd effect of disarming her. She sat up, straddling him, both of them still dressed. But even with their clothing between them, the feel of his hardness against her opening was almost more than she could bear. *Now.* She wanted him now, but she wanted to stretch this moment out, too, make it last forever.

She stayed still and just watched him for a second or two, drank in the sight of him. Laughter danced in his eyes and on his face, a lightness that drew her, that made her feel as though she didn't have a care in the world, that anything was possible.

She smoothed her hands over the rolling muscles of his chest then down his flat abdomen.

She'd thought that some day in the future she might make a friend. And maybe after they had years of becoming really comfortable, the friendship would quietly slip into something more. She had thought of a tender, healing kind of love.

She had never expected to be here on a bed, laughing and playing tickle with someone she'd met less than a week ago. She stilled for a moment. Where was her grief? Was she betraying Ian?

Danny watched her and grew serious. "Are you okay?"

He lifted his hands to her waist, his warm palms heating her through the fabric of her pajamas. His eyes held a sea of tenderness, openness. He understood.

Her body hummed with the desire he had awakened in her.

"Yeah, I'm okay," she said. And she was.

He was an unexpected turn in her life, but he was also right. She would have been lying to herself if she said otherwise.

She bent to him slowly and touched her lips to his, felt them stretch into a smile.

"Fair warning. To the winner go the spoils," she murmured against the corner of his mouth.

"Well then, if you must." He sighed dramatically. "Take me."

She did.

"I don't suppose you have any protection," he asked sometime later when they were both naked and ready to explode.

She shook her head. "I decided a while ago that I would probably never have sex again."

"That's a good resolution, Congresswoman." He dipped his head between her legs and sent her over the edge.

"But I think between the two of us," he said after he came up, while she was still contracting deep inside. "We should be able to come up with one that's much better."

By morning, he had made love to her just about every way he safely could, and he promised to do the rest at the earliest opportunity.

And she was pretty sure that what Daniel DuCharme promised, he would deliver.

"You know, men fall in love differently than women," he said as she was taking her time waking up in his arms.

"Mmm." Her brain was still swimming in a haze of pleasurable dreams.

"It's more of an instant thing, left over from the hunting-gathering days. A guy saw a deer, wanted it, went after it until he got it—instant decision-making."

"You want to go hunting? You should ask Cal."

"I'm talking about love."

That woke her up. "No," she said and pulled away. She wasn't ready for that discussion. She had to figure things out for herself first.

"I want to play it straight. I could see myself falling in love with you, Kaye."

Her heart tumbled. She panicked. "You can't. It's a crush."

"I'm a man, not a teenager."

Didn't she know it. "I can't handle this right now."

He watched her for a long time. "Okay."

"Okay, what?" she asked, bewildered, as she scampered out of bed with the sheet wrapped around her.

"I'm not going to push. I'm willing to wait," he said, then added, "to a point."

KAYE WATCHED the half dozen Secret Service agents who manned the room, each responsible for the feed of four security cameras. They kept a close eye on their split screens, talking into their headsets now and then. There were more agents on the receiving end, the ones who carried the hidden cameras through the crowd and moved in closer if anyone at command center requested.

"That's pretty good," she said. Of course, it had to be. Historically, one out of every four presidents had been attacked, one out of ten killed.

The large room had been set up by the advance team just for this day, on the sixth floor of a hospital that had gone out of business a year ago. In the back corner, there was still an X-ray light box on the wall. With the exception of a handful of relics, the rest of the room was jam-packed with top-of-the-line surveillance equipment.

"I suppose you can see pretty much everything from here." She spoke evenly, impersonally, as she would have to anyone. But her body was very much aware of Danny's nearness, of every little move he made.

He nodded. "This way, if we spot something suspicious, the target can be grabbed right then and there. With the long-distance cameras, by the time agents fought their way through the crowd, their man could be gone."

"Is that what those are?" She glanced to yet another row of screens to the right, monitored by the only other woman in the room.

"Rooftop cams." Danny stepped closer, putting her nerve endings on alert. "They can zoom in from as far as several city blocks, close enough to count the fingers on a man's hand."

Harrison came in, grabbed some equipment from a desk then walked out. Thank God the man had recovered. Probably not enough to be here, but he had insisted, and she didn't have the heart to say no. He had a giant chip on his shoulder about having failed to protect her before. He wanted desperately to prove himself.

A continuous stream of pictures scrolled down a giant screen beside her and drew her attention again, enlarged faces of individuals from the crowd outside.

"I've never been this close to the president's detail before. Impressive."

"Or disturbing. Depends on how you look at it." Danny shrugged. "There are all kinds of citizen groups protesting the cameras. A couple of cities are trying them for fighting crime."

She nodded, familiar with the privacy

issues that saw much discussion in Congress. Where was the line between preserving the right to privacy and keeping people safe?

"The walking cams are clearer." She looked between the two sets of screens, his nearness driving her crazy.

They hadn't had a chance to be alone since last night. How did he feel about it? Did he have any regrets?

Did she?

A million.

And yet, she wouldn't have changed a second of what had happened, not for the world.

"They fill in the blanks," he was explaining, as professional as could be. "The rooftop cams have limited coverage. They can't see around corners or behind street-vendor carts. That's where the agents come in. They can follow someone into a building, whatever."

"Whenever I'm inconvenienced by my security detail, I try to think of the president. Can you image this many people watching you twenty-four hours a day?"

He shook his head. "Wouldn't want the job."

She kept her attention divided among all the screens, although she had given descriptions of everyone she had seen at the compound. Danny had done the same. Now they watched and waited.

"Have you heard on the two guys we brought in?" she asked.

"They're not talking. Their lawyer is deliberately throwing up roadblocks to questioning. The bastards are playing for time. Wouldn't be surprised if the lawyer was in on this."

"Anything on Bobby Reznyck?" That was the name of the guy finally identified from the hospital video, the man who had kidnapped her.

"Still missing. He hasn't shown up for work in days, hasn't been back to his trailer." Danny sounded as frustrated as she felt. "Whatever's going down, it's going down here and now. The best we can do is to be prepared for anything."

And they were. Security on the street was massive. Blockades on every road except for the one on which the presidential motorcade would travel. The crowds were pushed back farther than usual. An increased number of uniformed and undercover security patrolled the area.

"There," Danny said suddenly and pointed to the screen. "See that guy?"

The agent responsible for that particular screen zoomed in on the man without having to be asked. "Stop," he spoke into his headset. "White male, dark blue jacket, short blond hair, straight ahead."

He didn't look familiar. "I don't know." Kaye ran through the images in her head, everything she'd seen at the compound.

"I'm going to take a closer look." Danny checked his gun then pulled his shirt back over it. "You stay put. You're safe here."

"Be careful."

"Always." He turned to the man in front of them. "Location?"

The agent on the street answered through the headset. "In front of Domino's Pizza," the desk man passed on the information.

Danny gripped an earpiece from the desk, clipped a microphone under his collar. "Sit here." He pulled a chair out for her and handed her a headset that was linked to the computer. He picked up a tiny button cam and stuck it over his top button, made sure it was steady. "Okay." He ran his fingers over the keyboard, pulled up some moving image that was out of focus and fuzzy. He adjusted the camera, and she was surprised to see herself on the screen. "This way you'll be able to see everything I do. You can talk to me through the headset. Sorry, all the cordless ones are individually assigned."

He adjusted the headset, smoothing her hair down, then let his hand run along her arm and squeeze her hand without anyone noticing. "I'll be back."

She could see every detail of the staircase, then the front door as he exited. Sunshine washed the picture white for a second, then the computer program automatically adjusted, adding contrast and making the feed darker for better visibility.

He moved through the crowd smoothly, the microphone picking up scraps of conversations.

"…she doesn't think like that. Very irresponsible…"

"…couldn't have. I know for sure…"

"…like hell. I'm gonna kill him."

The movement on the screen slowed as Danny stopped and looked over the woman who was talking. Mid-twenties, petite, average-looking.

"I'm not going to take his excuses anymore. Out with the guys, my ass. I know what he's doing when he doesn't get home till midnight…"

Danny moved on.

The next time he stopped, the screen showed the man he'd been looking for. Kaye didn't recognize him. She looked him over, her gaze hesitating on his right hand, stuffed deep in his pocket.

Danny was standing a few feet to the side. The man hadn't noticed him yet.

"Excuse me." She heard another's man voice. "Do you know what time it is?"

A well-dressed middle-age gentleman was talking to their target. His voice came through her headphone with an echo. She was hearing it twice, both from his microphone and Danny's. He was probably the agent whose button cam had first picked up the man.

"No," the guy said without moving his hand.

The agent asked a nearby group of teenagers. They were more accommodating.

"Thanks, guys," he said and settled into a spot not far from the man they were watching.

She could see the agent on the edge of the screen. Danny's camera was focused on their target.

"Is it him?" she asked.

"I'm not sure," came the low response. "Down in the gorge it was hard to see."

The man moved, turning into the crowd and walking toward the back. Danny followed. Now and then when he turned and the camera panned, she could see the other agent going with them.

"Excuse me, Congresswoman, could I ask you for a moment?" Harrison was standing behind her chair.

She'd been so focused on the screen,

she hadn't seen him walk up. "Of course." She stood and pulled the headset off. The cord reached only a few feet. "How are you?"

His lips thinned as he pressed them together. "Fine. There's nothing wrong with me. Even the headache is gone."

She wished she hadn't asked. He probably didn't like to be reminded. The only sign of his injury now was the small bandage that covered the stitches on the side of his head. He moved toward the door and she followed him.

"They said it was a bad concussion."

"That was days ago." He sounded impatient, very much like Danny who had, of course, also refused to be pulled from active duty. "One of our agents pulled a man off the street. He fits your description. Would you mind taking a quick look to confirm?"

"I am here to help."

"You won't even have to be in the same room with him. We'll just walk by the glass door."

They took the elevator down to the first level.

"This way." Harrison walked through a set of metal doors.

They were in some kind of an abandoned storage area, littered with metal and plywood shelving that reached to the ceiling. Dust covered everything, twitching her nose.

"Hang on. Let me see if they're ready for you." He walked across the large room and went out the door on the other side.

She looked around while she waited. It seemed such a waste to have all these huge buildings stand abandoned while in the inner cities thousands of homeless people slept on the streets—an issue she had addressed in D.C. with very little success. They needed better incentives for socially responsible corporations. Maybe once this was all over she could try again.

She touched a shelf and the dust made her sneeze.

"Gesundheit," a voice said behind her, and she spun around, startled, stared at the man who had appeared out of nowhere. "You scared me."

He came closer, his boots scuffing on the floor. His clothes looked worn and not entirely clean, as did his black hair and the stubble on his cheeks that had to be at least a few days' growth.

"I'm waiting for Mr. Harrison," she said, a little jumpy, not liking the shifty look in the man's watery green eyes.

Was he another agent? She must have met a hundred, coming and going all morning at the command center, waiting for the president's arrival. This one wasn't wearing his tag. Within the building, even the undercover officers had to wear one.

She stepped back, her instincts prickling. "I'm supposed to ID someone." Where was Harrison?

"Oh, we think you've done quite enough, Congresswoman," the man said.

And then finally the voice clicked, and she knew without a doubt where she had heard it before, where she'd seen that face— with blond hair and without the beard.

At the hospital.

Bobby.

She turned and ran for the door, her heart in her throat. A few more feet. Almost there. She slammed against it, but it held. *Locked.* She banged on the metal.

"That's no use. There's just the two of us here," the man said behind her.

She spun around, searched the room for any possibility of escape. "There are dozens of agents in the building."

"Not on this level." He flashed a smug grin. "The three guarding the elevator and the front and back entries have been called away."

"Mr. Harrison will be back in seconds." She skirted the wall, hoping to put a few rows of shelves between herself and the man.

He pulled his gun casually. "Lucky he wasn't seriously hurt the night your house was broken into."

What was he saying? Harrison couldn't have anything to do with this. She knew Harrison. Harrison had kept her safe.

"If he was working for you, he could

have killed me himself. He'd had plenty of opportunity." She inched back.

"He couldn't blow his cover, could he? Took us a while to get a man into a position with that high a clearance. We've got all kinds of plans for his future. You were just the beginning." He sneered. "Not even that. More like an unexpected detour."

Adrenaline was rushing through her, making her jumpy. She made a point of acting as calmly as possible. *Slow measured movements. Make the man think you're accepting his victory, make him think you've given up, then when his guard is down fight back with everything you've got.* Danny's words were coming back to her from one of their training sessions. She would stay calm. She could do it.

Then the man pulled back what she figured was the safety on the gun, and her resolution went out the non-existent window. She ran for the back of the room and dove for the protection of the shelves.

Harrison was one of them. The thought ricocheted through her head. She refused to give in to the sense of panic and betrayal.

"Let's not drag this out." He was coming closer. "I've got other things to do."

"It's not going to work." She had to distract him, rattle him enough to make a mistake. "Secret Service knows all about your plans for today. Why do you think they have all the extra security?"

He laughed. "It's not going to make any difference. We know they know."

Of course they would. Harrison. She had trouble getting her brain around that. It was impossible, wasn't it? Nobody had ever infiltrated the Secret Service before. Or, apparently, not that they knew of.

Could she have known? Had there been signs?

The pop of the first shot made her cringe. She forced her limbs to keep moving.

"In a few minutes our misguided president will realize just how much the people of this country object to his selling us out. America should be for Americans."

"I'm American," she said.

"Not in my book."

The second bullet slammed into the concrete floor just a few feet from her.

She could have pointed out that her grandfather's ancestors had been dragged into this country by force—kidnapped—and hadn't simply floated in on a pleasure cruise and decided to stay for the amusement of it. Her grandfather's family might have been in the country longer than his. But she understood the situation enough to know that reasoning with the man would be pointless. He'd been brainwashed too much for that. Fanatics had little use for logic or truth. She searched the floor for anything she might use as a weapon. She had to let him get close enough—without getting shot—so that she could fight back.

Her fingers closed around a two-foot-long metal bar, a fallen piece of shelving. Somehow she would have to disable him, then make a run for the other door, pray that it wasn't locked.

The shelves towered above her like benevolent giants. Bobby was on the other side somewhere. That gave her an idea.

She got up and leaned against the shelf in front of her, putting her full strength into the effort. The structure swayed. She pushed harder then pulled back. Maybe rocking would do the trick. She pushed again, every muscle in her body burning. The metal cut into her shoulder. It didn't matter. Harder. Now.

The first shelf fell over, but was caught by the second, they stood for a moment before giving way and pushing into the third.

Unfortunately, the domino effect stopped after the fifth row. A dozen or so standing shelves remained between her and Bobby.

"Let's get this over with." He squeezed off another shot.

The bullet ricocheted off a metal support just a few inches from her face. How could he see her in this jumble?

She moved forward, crawling on her stomach. The door was less than a hundred yards away. Eighty. Sixty. She pulled forward a few more feet, then reached the edge of her cover. From here she'd be out in the open.

She couldn't see Bobby.

With a little luck, he'd gone to the back to look for her and didn't realize where she'd gone.

She came up into a crouch and ran for it, grabbed onto the doorknob and twisted, pulled, rattled. How could it be locked? Had Harrison gone around?

"Game over," Bobby said behind her.

She spun around and stared at the gun in his hand. He was five or six feet away, ready to shoot her point-blank.

"Don't do it." She looked into his eyes, hoping to see some hesitation.

There wasn't any.

"You've climbed too far. It's not right."

Time slowed. She registered his body tensing as he got ready to pull the trigger.

No rules. Never give up. There's no such thing as a hopeless fight.

She threw the metal rod at him as hard as she could, diving forward at the same time.

The attack must have surprised the man because the shot went wide.

Then her head connected with Bobby's stomach and the next moment they sprawled, the gun skittering out of reach on the cement floor.

She got in one good punch to the face before he flipped her and had his hands around her throat. He wasn't messing around. The pressure on her windpipe was overwhelming, her lungs burning as he struggled against him.

The eyes.

She went for them without hesitation, didn't look to see what damage she'd done when he howled. She focused on her follow-up.

Refill the lungs.

Knee to the groin.

Shove him off.

He was trying to roll away from her. No, not from her. He was going for the gun. And he was closer to it. She slid in and kicked the weapon across the floor, under the shelving, the second before he would have reached it. He was grabbing for her ankle, but she shoved him off and made a run for the gun.

How far could it have gone? She scanned the rows one after the other. The weapon was midway in the fifth or sixth row, right where her shelf domino had stopped. She rushed between the rows without hesitation. He was right behind her.

She dove for the gun and reached it, spun around and squeezed off a shot blindly. She didn't hit him, but he jumped back, knocking into the shelves behind him. They groaned, rocking and creaking.

With everything she had in her, she ran toward the end of the row. He was swearing at her and following, but not fast enough. He didn't realize what was happening.

She flew out the end and sprawled on the floor just as the shelves toppled over, sandwiching Bobby's body between them. He screamed once, high-pitched and long. Then he gave no other noise.

Kaye ran for the door. Could she break the lock? The gun. She was still holding it. She shot at the lock a couple of times then kicked hard. Then she was through the door and out in the hallway, running for the elevator.

No. Bad idea. She turned. She couldn't go back up there to command central.

Harrison was up there somewhere. He would stop her.

Danny. Danny was just a few hundred feet down the street.

For a second she considered keeping the gun then discarded the idea and tossed it into the waste bin by the door. This was not a good day for running out into the street with a weapon. If Secret Service saw it, they might take her out before they realized who she was. She had to look disheveled enough to be a madwoman.

Kaye ran for the main entrance and burst outside, drawing attention from passersby. She straightened her clothes and did her best to act like a normal person in a hurry instead of someone either insane or dangerous.

She ran toward the corner where she'd last seen Danny on the monitor. How long did they have to stop the attack on the presidents?

*In a few minutes…*Bobby had said.

What were a few minutes? Ten? Fifteen? Five?

Could she still make it?

Chapter Ten

"Congresswoman?" Danny talked into his headset, standing apart from the crowd.

He was heading back to the building. The man he had pursued and caught had turned out to be a harmless bystander.

"Congresswoman Miller is with Harrison," one of the agents told him from the command center.

"She left?"

"A few minutes ago."

"Do you know where they went?"

"I'm not sure."

He looked toward the building. As long as she was with Harrison, she would be fine. Maybe the man had some questions for her.

He turned back toward the hotel. Movement caught his eye at the other end of the street. The presidential motorcade was finally coming. The police motorcycles first, then a cop car. The Secret Service vehicle was just turning the corner next. Some people in the crowd cheered, others booed. Opinions over the summit were pretty much divided.

The news reporters covering the event came to life, talking to their cameras.

He scanned the crowd, picking out the undercover agents one by one. Everyone was in place. He moved into the sea of people.

"Danny!" Somebody was calling his name from behind.

He looked back, but all he could see were the faces of strangers who paid little attention to him.

"Danny!"

Kaye? He pushed through the crowd, moving in the direction of the voice.

Then there she was, rumpled and her hair all out of place as if she'd been in a fight. He rushed to her and closed his arms around her without thinking. She put a hand over his mouth before he could ask what had happened, if she was all right.

She reached for the microphone under his collar with one hand and for the button cam with the other, shoved them into his pocket. "Turn them off." She mouthed the words.

He did so without questioning her.

"There is going to be an attack. Right now," she said.

"Everything is secured. Where the hell is Harrison?"

"Harrison is in on it."

He couldn't be. He was Secret Service. No organization had ever breached the agency before. But one look at Kaye's face told Danny she was dead serious.

Oh, hell. That meant the Brotherhood knew just how much security there was and where they were. "What are they going to do?"

"I don't know. But it's going to happen within minutes."

"And Harrison is hooked up to the system. We can't just call it in."

He moved toward the armed guards

who were holding the crowd back. The Beast, the black presidential vehicle that carried both President Derickson and Mexican President Alvarez to symbolize their unity over the Summit, was halfway down the street. They'd be stopping in front of the hotel soon.

What had the Brotherhood planned?

The Beast had state-of-the-art armor, its own supplemental oxygen supply and a self-healing fuel tank. It could drive even if the tires were shot out. The car was safer than some of the combat vehicles the army used around the world.

The bikes rolled closer, slowly, followed by the black and white. Then came the Secret Service car that carried some of the PPD, Presidential Protective Division, the agents who guarded the "Kill Zone"—the immediate area around the president. The Beast was next.

Danny pushed forward, his attention focused on the car. Then he saw something move. A small red dot hovered on the back of the rearview mirror.

"Oh, hell."

"What?" Kaye was right behind him.

"Someone painted the car."

"Huh?"

"Military talk. There's a missile guidance transmitter aimed at the mirror. See the small dot? Someone is keeping the laser on the car and transmitting exact location."

"To what?"

"My guess would be a big weapon they have stashed out of sight. This way, whoever fires the weapon doesn't have to be in direct view of the target and risk discovery, doesn't have to worry that he'll miss. His partner is 'painting' the target for him, communicating directly to the weapon."

She still looked somewhat confused, but he didn't have time for further explanations. He had to find the man who held the transmitter.

Couldn't have been anyone in the crowd. He scanned the surrounding buildings. They'd been checked over and over again. The advance team had spent the last five days securing the site, checking for potential sniper positions or anything else that was remotely suspicious. They set up safe houses along the way, brought in the president's own blood supply. All standard procedure. When the president was outside the White House, he traveled in a protective bubble. But this time, the bubble had been breached. The Brotherhood had someone on the inside.

He glanced back toward the command center, straight ahead of the limo that still hadn't progressed into the safety of the garage. Somebody moved on the roof. There was a guard posted there, but the last he'd seen the man he was in full military gear including a helmet. He didn't see a helmet on the guy up there now.

"Harrison," Kaye and he said at the same time and took off running.

They didn't have long before the presidential car would come to a stop. According to the schedule, the windows would roll down for about sixty seconds and the presidents would wave to the crowd. Then the limo was supposed to proceed to the underground parking garage that was fully secured.

Harrison was waiting for that sixty-second window to see the presidents and make sure they were indeed in the car and the whole thing wasn't faked as a last-minute security precaution. It had been done before. The PPD could have done it without telling the rest of the team.

Danny swore. If he broke radio silence to warn anyone, Harrison would signal for the hit. The only way to stop him was to catch him—now. The motorcade was moving slowly, but they didn't have long before it reached its location. Two minutes maybe, three at the most.

They ran through the front doors of the building. Kaye stopped for a second to reach into the garbage bin and came up with a gun.

What the hell? "Where did you get that?"

"Long story. Stairs or elevator?"

"Stairs," he said. Harrison had everything planned out pretty good. There was a chance that the elevator was rigged. If it were him up on that roof, he wouldn't want people to get to him in a hurry.

They took the stairs three at a time.

When they got to the sixth floor, they found a guard down, shot through the head. Blood pooled under his body.

"You should get off here, go to the secured room and wait." He stepped over the guy.

"No." Kaye followed him.

"I don't have time to argue."

"Then don't."

They pushed on, running up another two flights of stairs before reaching the door to the roof. Locked. Danny swore as he took the safety off his gun. They didn't have time to worry about whether or not they were making noise.

"You stay back here." He handed her the microphone from his pocket. "If anything happens to me, call for help. The guys in the command center will hear you."

He didn't wait for her answer. He kicked open the door and stepped out onto the roof.

THE ADRENALINE that washed through her veins was pushing her to go after him to help. Her brain was telling her she would be a liability. But she couldn't just stand there. She had to do something.

Kaye ran back down the stairs. They couldn't alert Secret Service over the radio just yet, not without tipping off Harrison. But she could alert them in person. Danny had been right. She should have gone there instead of coming up here with him. In the rush of the moment she hadn't had a chance to think it over, to reason it out. She'd simply followed her instincts that screamed "stick with Danny."

She flew down the stairs and over the dead man's body to the door that led to the hallway. She put a finger to her lips as she stepped out, signaling to the guard not to acknowledge her out loud.

She walked into the room the same way, straight to the wipe-off board, and wrote two words on it. *Radio silence*.

The agents hesitated. She gave them her best Majority Whip glare and added one more word. *Now!*

One by one, the men and the single female agent turned off their microphones.

"Harrison is on the roof. There's a laser-guided missile somewhere in the city. He's painting the presidents' car."

To their credit, no one questioned the veracity of her words, even though she was accusing one of their own. They were too well-trained to waste time on argument. Instead, the agents sprung to action.

"Daniel DuCharme is up there, trying to take Harrison down," she added.

One of the agents was typing furiously on his keyboard. "Give me a sec, then you can turn on the mikes. Maintain radio silence until you hear the all clear from me."

She moved over to him as the others left. "Can you do anything to cut Harrison off?"

The man nodded. "He has mike number twenty-one in our restricted radio network." He pushed the enter key. "There. He's out of the loop." He pulled the mouthpiece of his headset nearer his lips. "All clear. You may open communications."

Next, he relayed all the pertinent information to the choppers and the agents on the street. He was interrupted by the sound of gunfire from the roof above them.

"I'm going up." Kaye ran for the door.

He was in front of her long before she got there.

"I'm sorry, Congresswoman, but there's no way I can let you do that."

DANNY SQUEEZED OFF a shot then ducked behind the vent stack. A dozen agents were spreading out on the roof. Kaye had gotten word to the command room. Trouble was, he'd given her his mike, so he couldn't make contact with them.

He'd already shot the missile guidance transmitter out of Harrison's hand, but the man still had his gun, and from the look of things, he had a top of the line bullet-proof vest and no shortage of bullets. The heavy aluminum case of the vent he was leaning against had been riddled with them.

The sound of choppers filled the air. The enemy was defeated, they just didn't know it yet.

He had to get behind Harrison. Danny ran for the next vent, keeping low, dodging bullets.

THE AGENT was right. He was just doing his job. He was making perfect sense—an untrained civilian had no place in the middle of an armed confrontation. Still, it wasn't easy for Kaye to accept her uselessness.

The noise of the helicopters circling above drowned out every other sound.

"What's going on up there?" She looked toward the ceiling.

The agent tapped his earpiece. "Hard to tell, lots of yelling. I wouldn't—"

His words were cut off as the door banged open.

"Bobby." Kaye froze, her brain going blank. The man was dead. The shelves had fallen on him. What was he doing here? Then she recovered enough to think of running, and glanced around, desperate. In the small room there was nowhere to run.

The agent came out of his chair, went

for his gun. Too late. Bobby had his ready and he was a good shot. The man fell with a hole in the middle of his forehead.

"You thought you could take me out, bitch?" Bobby turned his attention to her. His right eye was bleeding, a gruesome sight, dried blood mixing with fresh on his face. His left arm appeared to be broken. There was blood on his leg, too, where something sharp had ripped his pants and his flesh.

The gun she'd taken off him earlier was on the computer desk behind her. She went down, swiping for it, took the security off as she'd seen him do and squeezed off a shot at the same time as he did. Then she dropped and rolled, just as Danny had taught her.

The man stopped moving and looked at her as if he was terribly surprised by this audacity. And then he fell like a log, face first, his head hitting the floor just a few inches from her.

"Kaye?" Danny stood in the doorway, gun in hand, his face white. "Are you okay?"

"I shot him." Her whole body felt numb all of a sudden.

"Well done," he said as color slowly returned to his cheeks. "I thought—" He didn't finish the sentence.

She came up to a sitting position, keeping her eyes on Danny, not wanting to look at the body. "I wouldn't have thought I could do it."

He came over and sat down next to her without touching her.

She took a deep breath. She wanted to get out of the room, but she didn't trust her legs to stand. "I didn't want to kill him. I just wanted him to stop."

"If it makes you feel any better, I got him, too. We both did."

She barely heard his words. She thought of all the impassioned speeches she had given on curbing violence. "What kind of a person does this make me?"

"A woman nobody better mess with." He put an arm around her and pulled her to him. "You're probably in shock. It's over, Kaye."

She heard his words, but couldn't quite comprehend them.

One of the agents came in, then another. Danny helped her up and moved away smoothly, making it all look professional.

"To hell with it," she said and moved back into the circle of his arms. She needed his strength and the comfort he gave.

From the corner of her eye, she could see as the chin of one of the agents just about hit his chest. The other turned away, giving them privacy.

Danny squeezed her and placed a kiss on the top of her head then raised his gaze and talked to the men. "How are the streets?"

"Closed off," one of them said then called in their fallen colleague, while the other took the man's place at the controls. The president was still on location. They had a job to do.

She clung to Danny and he made no move to let her go. "I need a chopper on the roof in five minutes. I'm taking Congresswoman Miller off site," he said.

"Yes, sir." The man made the request over his radio.

The next thing she knew, she was swung into Danny's arms as he carried her out of the room.

Agents were walking down the hallway.

"Are you all right, Congresswoman?"

"She's fine." Danny kept going.

"I can walk," she told him half-heartedly.

"I know. But I badly want to touch you, and this is the only way I can think of doing it without causing a complete scandal," he whispered back.

She put her arms around his neck. "Do I look like I'm worried about it?"

He took a long look at her as he walked to the staircase and started up.

There were still agents coming from the roof. "Need any help?"

"Everything is under control. Minor injuries." Danny passed by them on his way up. "No, you don't look worried," he said after a minute, then he stopped.

And then he kissed her.

She was dimly aware of people passing them, a low wolf whistle coming from somewhere. She didn't care. The only thing she could think of was that they were both alive, that she was in Danny's arms.

He pulled away, touched his forehead to hers before moving on. "Sorry. I really needed that."

"Me, too," she said.

"You're not making this easier for me." He grinned.

"Am I supposed to?"

"Hell, yes. You keep up with this and it's going to be pretty difficult for me to become the Speaker's secret lover."

Her lover. Her heart thumped at the words as her brain turned them over.

They reached the roof just as the last of the agents were clearing out.

Her lover. "Is that what you want?" she asked when they were alone.

He looked her deep in the eyes, the ever-present grin gone from his face. "I want a hell of a lot more, Kaye, but I'm aware of your position. I'll take whatever I can get."

"But—"

"I want it all. I want everything. I love you."

"It's not that I don't want to—"

"You don't have to explain anything to me."

"Everything happened so suddenly. I didn't expect— I just—" She wanted so badly to make him understand, but for once she wasn't sure what to say. "It's crazy. I'm falling in love with you." Frustration pushed the words from her, and she froze as soon as they were out, surprised by them, unsure what to say next.

He took in a slow breath then let it out. "About time. I think I've been in love with you since the day you beat me up in your basement."

"I did not beat you up. You were training me."

"I'm thinking you should maybe have a little more training. There are a couple of self-defense moves best demonstrated by rolling on the mat."

"Self-defense is important," she said. "But maybe I need stronger measures, considering what's happened in the last couple of days."

He nodded solemnly. "Should be watched 24/7."

"How closely?" she asked.

"As closely as possible."

"Know any volunteers?"

"I might," he said. "Tell me again."

"I love you, Daniel DuCharme."

Epilogue

"I can't believe *we* are in the Lincoln Bedroom." Kaye glanced around as she kicked off her high heels, her gaze lingering over the slim posts of the gorgeous bed, the antique linens, the chandelier.

Their reward for saving the lives of two presidents was kept low key since Danny was part of a secret military unit. The media couldn't very well paste his face all over the news and explain who he was and what he was doing at the Summit. The official story credited Secret Service with saving the day.

But there had been a number of rewards for the two of them, such as dinner at the White House that evening.

"It was nice of Derickson to ask us over." Danny grinned at her.

He was leaning against one of the bed posts, wearing a tuxedo like the first time she'd seen him. He looked impossibly handsome with that sexy smile hovering over his lips, his gaze boring into hers.

"He is still upset over Harrison." She flexed her toes, glad to be rid of the shoes. "So am I."

The president had given them an update when the topic came up. Harrison was finally talking. He'd been unhappy at the agency, hadn't been promoted as he thought he should be. He'd been waiting for the last ten years to get onto the president's detail. Others had made it before him, some of them minorities. When The New Brotherhood tempted him through his new girlfriend, he let himself be swayed by his own resentment and their money.

Even now, he did not see his acts as betrayal of his oath. He was convinced he was doing his best to save his country.

She reached to her nape, to the back of her gown to pull down the zipper.

"Let me." Danny strode to her.

She turned and pulled a few loose tendrils of hair out of his way.

"So much of life is coincidence," she mused. "If Bobby Reznyck didn't get fixated on me and decide to pursue his own agenda within the Brotherhood, I would have never met you, never have found out about the planned attack on the Summit."

"He was obsessed with you. He blamed everything that had gone wrong in his life on some law you voted on years ago."

His voice was thick with barely restrained anger that told her Bobby Reznyck was lucky he would spend the rest of his life in prison. He wouldn't want to run into Danny.

"But if it's all the same to you, I'd prefer if you didn't refer to our meeting as *coincidence*," he added. "That was fate."

He tugged the zipper down slowly, gently. When he was done and the fabric gaped open, he drew a finger down her naked back.

Heat pooled inside her. And need.

He brushed the straps down her shoulders, nudged them along until the sky blue silk pooled at her feet. He turned her and dragged his lips over hers once, twice, then, leaving her aching for more, moved back to allow her room to step out of the dress.

"I love you," he said.

She went to him, lifting her arms to wrap them around his waist, but he captured her hands and kissed her palms in turn, long and hot, before letting them on their way.

Amazing how little it took for him to send her insides melting. She glanced around, self-conscious given the historical significance of the room. "If these walls could talk—"

"They would say: Kiss him already." He pulled her even closer until their lips met.

He felt incredible. She forgot all about their surroundings when he deepened the kiss.

And he didn't stop there. In a smooth move, he maneuvered her forward a few steps, then pulled her down to the bed, on top of him.

"So you think Cal is warming to the idea

of the two of us together?" he asked when they came up for air.

"He better."

They'd had a long talk when he'd gotten back from his "golf vacation." Seeing him come back whole and safe had been a tremendous relief. She had a good inkling that he was involved in the same thing as Danny, that he was the boss, that every time one of them went away on a "consulting assignment" they went to combat, to mortal danger.

She wondered if she would ever get used to that. Maybe not get used to, but she could and would accept it. Because these were the two men in her life whom she loved beyond all others. And she wasn't powerless. She would do her best in her own position to make the world a safer place.

"He still gives us separate rooms when we come to dinner and end up staying the night," Danny remarked.

"He's an old fashioned man."

"There goes my plan of eloping in Vegas." He took a deep breath and held her gaze. "I suppose I'm going to have to ask him for your hand in marriage, all proper."

Her breath hitched. She couldn't keep the smile from her face and the tears from her eyes. She hadn't thought she would marry again, that she could love again. But what she'd found with Danny was a pure and generous blessing, if unexpected. And she was determined to hold on to that treasure, not to let anything or anyone between them.

"I love you Daniel DuCharme," she pressed her lips to his, and sunk into his heat and into the happiness he'd brought to her life.

* * * * *

Look for Dana Marton's next gripping romantic suspense when BRIDAL OP, part of Harlequin Intrigue's four-book series MIAMI CONFIDENTIAL, debuts in August 2006.

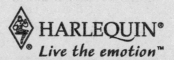

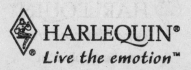

Harlequin Historicals®
Historical Romantic Adventure!

*From rugged lawmen and
valiant knights to defiant heiresses
and spirited frontierswomen,
Harlequin Historicals will
capture your imagination with
their dramatic scope, passion
and adventure.*

*Harlequin Historicals . . .
they're too good to miss!*

HARLEQUIN®
Presents

The world's bestselling romance series...
The series that brings you your favorite authors,
month after month:

Helen Bianchin...Emma Darcy
Lynne Graham...Penny Jordan
Miranda Lee...Sandra Marton
Anne Mather...Carole Mortimer
Susan Napier...Michelle Reid

and many more uniquely talented authors!

Wealthy, powerful, gorgeous men...
Women who have feelings just like your own...
The stories you love, set in exotic, glamorous locations...

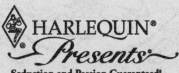

HARLEQUIN®
Presents

Seduction and Passion Guaranteed!

HPDIR104